Black Rainbow

Paperback original

ALSO BY PHILIP CALLOW

NOVELS
The Hosanna Man
Common People
A Pledge for the Earth
Clipped Wings
Going to the Moon
The Bliss Body
Flesh of Morning
Yours
The Story of My Desire
Janine
The Subway to New York
The Painter's Confessions
Some Love
The Magnolia

SHORT STORIES
Native Ground
Woman with a Poet

BIOGRAPHY
Son and Lover: The Young D.H. Lawrence
Van Gogh: A Life
Walt Whitman: From Noon to Starry Night
Lost Earth: A Life of Cézanne
Chekhov: The Hidden Ground

AUTOBIOGRAPHY
In My Own Land

POETRY
Turning Point
The Real Life
Bare Wires
Cave Light
New York Insomnia
Icons
Soliloquies of an Eye
Fires in October
Nightshade and Morning Glory

Black Rainbow

Philip Callow

Shoestring Press

Black milk of dawn we drink you at dusk . . .

Paul Celan

Typeset by The Midlands Book Typesetting Company, Loughborough (01509 210920)
Printed by Quorn Selective Repro, Loughborough (01509 213456)

Published by Shoestring Press
19 Devonshire Avenue, Beeston, Nottingham NG9 1BS.
Telephone: (0115) 925 1827

First published 1999
© Copyright: Philip Callow, 1999
ISBN 1 899549 33 1

Shoestring Press gratefully acknowledges financial assistance from
East Midlands Arts.

PART ONE

LOST IN THE FIELDS

Chapter One

He supposed he was old; and went on regardless. At fifty-nine he hadn't felt old, or even thought it. He turned sixty and at once thought it, but without caring. He'd stopped shaving; it became a beard, black and grey mixed. Now he rarely saw himself in a mirror. Never before a Bible reader, he found a sentence in Isàiah and jotted it down: 'The wilderness and the solitary place shall be glad for them.' He combed his hair with hooked fingers usually, since there was no one to approve or disapprove. Worse, no one to please.

To be old in England, someone said, was to be shunted into a siding and forgotten. That's it, that's what I want; so I'll be old, he thought. No one admits to being outcast, let alone welcomes it. I do; it's my shameless dream. The idea had come stealing into him, first of all as a thought, a wish, then gradually mounting to a steady insistent yearning, that what he would like more than anything was some way of just walking off and leaving the world. Who would miss him? If there was only a gate you could quietly walk through and disappear, out of sight of the world. He went around hugging this desire in secret, unwilling to confide it to anyone – not that there was anyone – until he realised it wasn't simply a means of consoling himself. No, he meant it. Then he got practical: he went deliberately looking for a hiding place.

He had been sixty for a week. He was keeping a diary for the first time in his life. Did he mean a journal? Anyway, a log of his days, of a solitude of days and nights. The idea of a journal had always appealed, but living for posterity seemed fatuous. Also he lacked patience. It was something others did, not him. Now he had endless time, and to try to account for it, make sense of it, justify it even, seemed right. It might even redeem the black something stuck immovably in his chest. He was unable to say more. Unwilling maybe.

Then he knew. He would talk to his wife in it, constantly, incessantly, even though he would never see her again in this life. It occurred to him that he was out to convince himself that he still lived. Did he? After the smash, for a long time he had no interest in living. He wouldn't touch a car, went everywhere on foot. Afterwards he was a ghost in the world; he conversed with ghosts. Having to pretend that life went on as usual was a howling farce, so he buried himself away here. Nobody here knew his history. If he could he'd erase his name. People here, mercifully few in number, were no more to him than the sheep and cattle on the hills, the pigs rooting peacefully outside his back door a few yards away on the other side of the wire fence.

He was in the Cotswolds, sunk away up a long muddy drive, all potholes, between rows of poplars in the heart of the country; not a house in sight. He was no countryman, so he had always idealised fields and farms. Being in the country for him was like being on holiday – an escape from somewhere. What drew him to it in his dead condition was the emptiness, the blessed scarcity of people.

The advert in the Sunday paper spoke of a cottage, warm, well-equipped. 'Warm if you worked at it,' he thought wryly. As for well-equipped, it wasn't true. None of that bothered him in the least. To him it was a shelter, a retreat; a small stone house that was a kind of miniature of the grand stone farmhouse on three floors a little further on up the mud and shale, past the barns and outhouses. The great blowy barns with their corrugated roofs and flapping wood reeked of cows even when they were empty. Trudging past them to collect his milk he knew he was in foreign land, submerged in sounds and smells he had never lived with before.

Farmer Symonds was like no farmer he'd ever met. He spoke incisively, a person of some culture who was apparently unwell, mentioning this in every other remark, along with his contempt for the contemporary scene. Bristling with hostility, overbearing in spite of himself, he seemed genuinely distressed by injustice in general and the treatment of farm animals in particular. A pungent sense of humour, often only comprehensible to himself, spurted out of him from time to time. His features were large and squashed, scalded by the weather, with thick gone-to-seed tangled eyebrows. The wife, his opposite in every way, was sweet-tempered, quiet as milk, a profoundly deaf woman who came and went silently, greeting you with shy smiles. She reminded the new tenant of his saintly grandmother. He imagined Mrs S. putting her arm round him and saying, 'What is it, my duck?' If she had a voice, that is.

Symonds, instead of asking for references, probed for likes and dislikes, preferring to make up his own mind. His blunt approach was acceptable to the other's craven state.

'My memory's terrible,' he said, almost barked. 'Tell me your name again.'

'Hopkin. Matthew.'

'Married?'

The newcomer shook his head, though the answer was yes, always would be. Once married, forever married. A married man to the end. If he looked vague it was because Isaiah had floated into his head again: 'And man is bowed down and man is humbled.'

'How long did you say you wanted the cottage?'

'That depends.'

'Do you have a job?'

'I'm retired.'

'Know anything about organic farming?'

'No.'

'Fit, are you?'

'Yes.'

Suddenly the deal was clinched. Symonds extended his rough paw; cracked a smile. Startled, Hopkin stood up. Mrs S. entered silently from a side door of the large flagged kitchen, dominated by a huge Rayburn along one wall. She smiled at the stranger and went on, out through a rear door into the house somewhere.

'My wife,' Symonds said without looking. 'She's deaf.'

He cursed under his breath, rose stiffly from the table as though to ease pain in his back and stood over by the kitchen dresser. 'If you take the place for several months we'll adjust the rent accordingly,' he said through grimaces.

'Twelve months?'

'Better make it six. You might fall out with us. Or vice versa.'

'True,' the other said. It came out as amusement.

Symonds stared belligerently. 'I'm serious.' He came back and sat down again. Hopkin heard himself say, then wanting to bite his tongue, 'Thanks for your time.'

'Do you have a dog?'

'No.'

'Good. We don't allow them.'

'Anything else?'

'You drive I take it?'

'Yes, but I don't have a car.'

'Are you socialist?' he asked abruptly.

'I was once.'

Symonds was glaring somewhere over his head. 'No point in being anything else. With the government we've got, it's a matter of morals. I ask you. They lack all principles. How long have we had to suffer them?'

'I'll go and get settled in,' the tenant said, moving off.

'You like music?'

'Oh yes.'

'Paintings?'

'Some.'

'Poetry?'

'Certainly.'

The farmer stood up violently, gripping the edge of the table. Again he thrust out his hand. 'Then we'll get on.'

'Hope so.'

'You should find everything you need up there. Shout if you don't.'

'I'll pay a month in advance,' Hopkin began. Symonds waved him off. 'Later, later.'

He reflected that evening that he liked Symonds, that is if you could like someone impregnable like a wall. Leaving him he went out into the autumn mud and deepening dusk, glad to be alone again. Talking to anyone was a strain. All his conversations were interior ones and he resented it when they were interrupted. Outer ones jarred, hit his ears like notes from a bugle. He walked away down the farmyard of cow-pats and straw in long ropes, the ground rutted by tractors and trailers, the air heavy with the smell of dung, of a whole summer come to a halt and starting to rot.

In his strange cottage-house which had nothing to do with him he unpacked his few belongings. There was an old TV on a tea trolley. It had an indoor aerial. The picture was terrible. He tried the loop in various positions and then gave up, telling himself the company it offered was spurious. He switched on his radio and killed it at once. Sitting in an armchair with broken springs he looked at the cassettes he had brought, with nothing to play them on. It didn't matter. The silence in the place and outside, pressing on the windows, insisted on being heard. He went outside and stood in the immense country dark, rearing up on all sides, black as walls. He was at the back, facing a wood. It started to rain, and he heard it on the thousands of unseen leaves. He let himself back in, and after a while walked about, outwardly healthy but in poor shape within, thankful for the company of the sounds his feet made, as if they belonged to someone else. His dejection waited for him in all the corners. Melancholy could be pleasurable or like ashes, he told himself.

Upstairs in the biggest bedroom he stood at the window. A car went bumping past, wallowing in the holes, lights blazing. Then nothing. The window frame was silted with dead flies. He looked at the bed and fought a longing to lie down and sleep, so as to wake up in another day with at least a chance. This one had defeated him.

Downstairs he passed through the kitchen to the high lean-to conservatory with its floor of rough concrete and its enormous boiler, like the cylinder of a steam engine stranded on its side. It burned great baulks of timber and split logs which he could wheel in from the open-sided shippen a few yards up the drive. There was a wheelbarrow he could use. Pipes from this weird contraption provided hot water and central heating of a sort.

A mild night. Standing again on rank grass beyond the conservatory wall he listened to nothing, engulfed in dense black like a blind man. He heard the snuffling of pigs. Then again nothing. Deep in the wood close by an owl hooted once, an extraordinary soft tender sound, welling out of the dark. He stood like a post, telling himself that what he heard was the voice of the night itself.

Staying there for no other reason than that his legs had carried him to the spot, he thought, 'Should I go to bed?' If he did he would only lie in a wash of thoughts and memories, most of them desolate. There was something habit-forming about mournfulness. For so many nights he had curled up into it. Sleep came when you had given up all hope of sleeping.

It was two years now almost to the day since the smash. He walked about with his sound limbs and people must have thought he was undamaged. Nothing would be the same, but who was to know? He didn't want to adapt to what once was, now the heart was torn out of it. He had come here in the forlorn hope of changing his life. 'That's to say if I have one to change,' he thought. The old life was dead.

There was a strong musty smell in the bedroom. Before spreading his sheet he pressed his hand flat on the mattress. It felt dry enough. The earthy smell was up his nose, everywhere, faint but unmistakable even in the kitchen. After a while he stopped caring.

Under the duvet he thought of what he'd do tomorrow; never mind the next day and the next. A sane start would be to make a shopping list of essentials. Then for the march down the unsurfaced drive, at the road turning left to Stroud, four miles, dropping steadily for part of the way. He might look for a bike. In the other direction was a village they called Ash. The softness of the name made him want to go there. First though he needed to get his bearings. Nagging at him was a letter to his mother in Dorset whom he knew was waiting anxiously to hear from him. 'Oh mother, mother, look at your son,' he thought or said under his breath, but it came out aloud, a sad chant. He pictured his sad mother, alone as he was, bitterly unhappy and with no hope of changing anything now. Who knows, maybe it was the same for him. Jesus changed my life, they said, eyes shining, those he had once pitied as simpletons and now envied.

He was half asleep in his confused state, drifting off in broken water.

He woke with a racing heart. Somebody was in the cottage below him. The bedroom was pitch dark. Lying rigid and fearful he listened hard. Clanking noises; silence. Groping for a dressing gown he sneaked downstairs with a torch as if he was the thief.

'Hallo?'

A voice called, 'Sorry, it's me. I thought nobody was in.'

Going through the kitchen the fuddled man came face to face with a big figure, young, blocking the way to the conservatory. 'Sorry to disturb you. I looked in to see if you needed any help with the boiler. Usually they do. You haven't lit it yet, so I'll get it started for you if that's all right.'

'What time is it?'

The man glanced at his watch. 'Nine-thirty. I'm the son, by the way. Michael. You're Mr Hopkin.'

'Matthew.'

Michael Symonds: an intelligent handsome face, a boyish charm. Oxford graduate. Hopkin thought, this family is full of surprises, not really taking in rapid instructions for the care and operation for the boiler, which was French. To hear him talk you could imagine he was recommending the virtues of a person. As he spoke he kept poking bits of kindling through the open hatch into the thing's iron belly. He struck a match. After a few minutes he began loading up with split logs. 'It's splendid really, once you get the hang of it. We had it installed a year ago. You can pack it as full as you like before you go to bed and it should still be going next morning. Works better when it's packed. Know where your supply of fuel is?'

'Your father told me.'

'Right, I'll leave you in peace. Apologies again for barging in unannounced. Hope I didn't alarm you.'

'Puzzled me that's all.'

'Good. Sleep well.'

He went clumping off in his gumboots. Hopkin locked the door behind him and went back to bed. But now he was thoroughly awake. Someone was knocking on the side door.

It was Michael. He waved to Hopkin through the glass. The tenant let him in.

'No need to lock this, unless you want to, that is.'
'I'll remember.'
'I meant to explain about the valve.'
'Valve?'
'This one here, on the wall.'
'What's it for?'
Michael beamed. 'If you need more heat, open it full. Otherwise leave it half open as it is now.'
'Got it.'
'My father tells me you're a reader.' He hung forward, hanging his head.
'All my life, yes. Not so much now perhaps.'
'Books are addictive,' he said solemnly. 'Do you find that?'
'You could say a disease,' Hopkin said, venturing a smile.
Michael opened his mouth to launch into something, then cut it short. 'Must get on. Talk to you again I hope.'
Hopkin agreed in theory that they should, though he only nodded. He went to turn the key after the big fellow, stopped himself, and went back to bed.

It was another day. He got up dazed, as if hungover, and went down the slippery open staircase of polished wood slats in bare feet, feeling safer that way. Filling the kettle from the tap made an unearthly crash. The silence ran back. He switched on and then stood like an imbecile, spellbound, listening to the faint stir of the water around the kettle element as the heat entered. At the front window, holding his cup of tea, he looked out at the big messy drive, the barns, the coarse field tilting steeply upwards. No sign of life. He looked out at nothing.

He had brought a few books, which he put on a shelf and then ignored, as he did his old Olivetti portable. Somewhere on the way to here the clue to books had been lost. It was how he wanted it. Symonds had lent him a map of the area. He preferred not to open it, but instead to find out his way be degrees. It was an old instinct. On holidays abroad he would try to avoid tourist guides. Though he felt buried and nowhere like an old earth-man without a language he knew he was not lost: not here, not in England. Before coming he had read some letters by a man visiting Australia in the twenties. Over and over the traveller marvelled at the emptiness, and said at one point that if you wanted to withdraw from life altogether and cease caring about anything, the interior of Australia was the place. It was pre-history. Life hadn't properly begun there, it was peopled with ghosts, the souls of future centuries. 'Maybe I should have tried it,' Hopkin thought. Here there were presences in abundance, populating this intense living quiet.

He ate a bowl of cereals, then wrote a list for when he tramped down the road to Stroud. He had landed there on the country bus from Cheltenham, where he used to live in another life. When he came back from the shops he would write to his mother, who at eighty-two still saw him as a child. Her cottage was smaller than this place. She lived pressed around with old beams and thick damp walls. She would have been up for hours, simply because for her it was shameful to lie in bed when everyone was about their business. What if someone called? The curtains had to be drawn back or some busybody might think she was ill. When she was, it was with worry.

On the way down the red-earth, rubble-strewn drive between the gracefully waving poplars he met a man driving a tractor, pulling an empty trailer. He nodded briefly and went on.

In Stroud, a little town of narrow streets on very steep hills, he bought vegetables and fruit and bread, and found a stationer for paper and envelopes. There were several poky cafés and it made sense to have lunch there. The one he chose seemed to be run entirely by elderly ladies. The one who came for his order reminded him of his mother, but was much happier. She smiled when he decided on the quiche and baked potato, as if he'd given her pleasure. Was she simply pleased to be serving others? Everything that occurred now, all these first impressions he stored up half unconsciously to put in his letter afterwards, should he get around to writing it.

Coming out of Stroud on foot he began writing the day's journal entry in his head. Once you got into the habit this happened, whether the page was open in front of you or not. Until it was done you were under pressure. He had walked past a large house set back from the road, and from the bell pushes he saw it was in flats. To the journal in his head he told this, going on to confide that he was reminded of the rambling flat in the Georgian house in Cheltenham where he lived once with Lena, his wife. The house had peeling yellow stucco. It still had, though now his son and his family lived there. From its front windows you looked down on a railed and gravelled access road. Beyond the railings and shrubbery and the main road were the trees and shrubs of the little park in the middle of the square. All the residents of the square were entitled to a key. He had gone into this private garden only once, sitting down on a bench and trying to enjoy it. He felt stupid. Though he had a right to be there, somehow he was an intruder.

The house was on three floors. They were at the top. As he remembered, all the years there ran together. He ascended the three broad stone steps and went in, up the linoleum stairs, the stairwell that was never decorated, past the second floor flat with its nameplate, Holly, and on up to his, entering the narrow dog-leg corridor, sharp right past the kitchen and then the open space with doors opening off, two bedrooms and a big square living room. From the sash window in the kitchen you looked down on the overgrown garden in shadow from its high brick walls, one of them crumbling, bulging. A cat appeared there and vanished from time to time. That and the birds were the only signs of life. One year, new tenants moved in on the ground floor and a little girl ran up and down, clapping her hands suddenly and whirling on her heels to stare up at him.

He could see Lena there, calling him to the kitchen window. When he talked to her now in spirit it was there, preparing the meals and in a mess, absorbed in the quiet contentment she found in cooking.

Her daughter from a previous marriage, then their son – they turned the boxroom into a den for him – this was their cell of good living. It endured twenty-six years. Endured? The time flew by. Nobody mentioned boredom. What were their quarrels about? He couldn't remember. Why did she strike at him once, hitting him across the face in her rage, shaking all over? It was gone. They had lapses and then recovered, went on sanely and perhaps dully again. They were good friends, comfortable with each other. In the early years their desire was fierce, flamey. He would press her waist in the kitchen, she would sag into him a little. He would always want to fill his hands with her. Shy creatures, both of them, they escaped from the burden of themselves into each other's bodies. Arriving home from work, opening the silent door at the top of the stairs, he would rejoice in the mystery of their cloistered lives as he penetrated the secret domain of the long dog-leg corridor. Of course, he remembered, it was windowless, a blind channel leading to an inner sanctuary, to the womb their home was – how could he have forgotten?

Their desire guttered down with familiarity, an old story, flaring up to surprise them when they assumed it was extinct, gone for good. If only he could feel again the joy of that leaping into her and then the benediction, in the midst of such barrenness? So easy, so simple! Lena, his journal mourned, I was in pieces and you mended me. What did I do for you? Lena, I can't live like this. Come back. I am just a bundle of old memories. Wait for me.

Chapter Two

It surprised him, after nearly a month, to find he was still there and living the life of a hermit. Sometimes he felt absurd, a fraud. Who did he think he was, Thoreau? The man on the tractor who worked the Symonds land was another widower, he believed. The woman running the little shop in Stroud where he bought his eggs and cheese knew all about the farm he was living on. She was perhaps fifty, with quick, restless, startled-looking black eyes that went darting over his face. She liked to tell him things. 'One day she'll want my story,' he thought.

'There was a young lad living in your cottage before you,' she said.

'I don't know,' he said, misunderstanding.

'Good-looking boy. Agricultural student.'

'Did he stay long?'

'Three, four months. Then they threw him out.'

'What for?'

'Unreliable. Liked a good time. Took girls in. Hung around in the *Golden Hind* too much.'

'Lonely perhaps?'

'That's it. None of his company up there.'

'I suppose not.'

The woman wasn't finished. 'Mr Symonds is all right. I like him.'

'Me too. Though I hardly know him yet.'

'You don't mess with him. No fear.'

'What about his wife?'

'Joan. Lovely old soul.'

'Very different to him.'

'Like chalk and cheese them two.'

The *Golden Hind* became one of his dropping-in places. Unless he was unable to settle quietly at night he stayed in. Only once had he ventured out after dark. He might listen to music on the radio but he was choosy. Big orchestral sound he tended to avoid: it pounded at him, threatened to break in. He found it too emotional altogether. For the first time in his life he began to follow the intricacies of chamber music. He thought vaguely of buying a cassette player, of getting hold of some Beethoven sonatas. For years he had told himself to try the late quartets. He had heard once, in a Jacqueline du Pré concert on TV, Beethoven's *Ghost Trio*.

Maybe now was the time. It occurred to him that where he was now, not physically but inside himself, might make him more receptive to things of the spirit. The truth was that his body felt no more than a vehicle for getting him from one place to another. But he did nothing. The human voice, especially the chattering, asserting, opinionated voice, he switched off at once.

As October drew to a close and the night frosts began he heard the owl more often, hunting at night. Because it thrilled him he decided he was after all still in the world, if not of it. He thought of it as one owl, almost as his owl. It awoke awe in him, this unattainable creature, its call so tender and low, seductive. In ages past it symbolised death and also wisdom, he believed. Was he being serenaded from beyond the grave? He wanted desperately to think so. He stood on the threshold of his bleak cavernous conservatory, the massive bulk of the boiler filling the space behind him, hoping to hear his hunting owl. Often he was disappointed, but never wholly so. Let death hunt him down. The bristling dark wood looming up ahead of him, motionless on quiet nights, had been something so alien at first that he'd been glad to turn his back, shutting the door on it with the uneasiness of the nervy town dweller. Now it too was turning into a creature that touched him curiously, a little deeper each time, beginning to put its spell on him. All those trees waiting. It was another world. They all stood waiting, submitting to the approach of winter, waiting in a dim half-life, like him.

He had stopped going to the café of old ladies. Their kindliness and old-world charm were too much. They came fussing up to coddle him and he was thrown back into childhood, reminded painfully of his lonely, bitterly isolated mother, living for his phone call which now never came. He wrote instead; or he would write. He would have to go and see her soon. Breaking free again when he was there was something to be dreaded. Her pathos caused something in him which he badly needed to hang on to now to disintegrate, and if he was going to survive that was terrible. If he wanted to, that is.

He was at the mercy of sounds and faces, incidents that jogged memory, and for this reason he shrank back, hugged his solitude. Only the other day, heading for the *Golden Hind* with his rucksack of supplies to have a bite of lunch, intent on satisfying at the same time a furtive need for company, he heard a squeal of brakes that chilled his blood, bringing it back in a sickening flood. His heart and mind blackened. Not that he could recall squealing brakes. It was twilight, the worst time for drivers on unknown roads. He saw a shadow jump out in front of him – an animal was it? There had been rain for days, a layer of mud on the road. He braked, skidded, his nearside wheel sank in a ditch, he rammed a fence post, then another, capsized, ploughing along on the car side.

He was bleeding from lacerations to his forehead, his left arm useless. His wife had died instantly, her neck broken. Seconds before, she had reached back for her handbag. Had she unfastened her seat belt at that point? His first impulse in his rage at his loss was to seek out the paramedics and establish the truth. The thought – or was it survivor guilt? – shamed him and he did nothing.

He reached the pub and sat in a corner, shaken, looking white and strange, staring-eyed. The man nearest to him on the bench asked him if he was all right.

'Yes, fine,' he said, his unsteady voice betraying him.

'You need a strong drink,' the man said. 'Hang on.'

He went to the bar, called to the woman Elsie with easy familiarity and had a muttered conversation with her.

'Drink this,' he said to Hopkin, and put a brandy in front of him.

Hopkin reached for his money. The stranger stopped him. 'On me. You can get the next one.'

A log fire blazed in the gaping stone hole of the fireplace. The bar was filling up with locals, men who knew each other, shouldering in from the fields and workshops. The atmosphere was cheery, masculine, loud with the chafing outer noise that men generate when they are in their own company, away from women. It was a freemasonry Hopkin liked, though often he had felt excluded from it. This man beside him didn't seem to belong with the others. He sat quietly sipping his bitter.

Hopkin gagged on his spirits; his chest burned. 'Not my usual tipple,' he struggled to say between splutters.

'Brandy for courage,' the man said.

'I've heard that.'

'What we all need, wouldn't you say?'

'Brandy or courage?'

'Both.'

The man jumped up and left quickly, light on his feet, a small man in his forties. Hopkin had been preparing his own awkward excuses in order to escape, and he still sat there. He felt a ditherer. He went to the bar and ordered sandwiches and a coffee.

'Hot beef?'

'Please.'

He asked casually after the man who had just left. 'He bought me a drink,' he started to explain, but the woman had seen.

'That's Julian,' she said flatly. 'Can't tell you his other name.'

He pretended indifference, not wanting to sound over-curious. Somehow the man's tense, averted face had put Hopkin in mind of his friend Bill Walsh, though the stranger was younger. What was it? Both of them small men, but that wasn't it. Could it be a kind of darkness they trailed? Bill had been unhappy for years, under a cloud so permanent that it was hard to remember a time when he had been different. Intensely serious even when they first met, but always cracking up with laughter. At eighteen his introspection was well hidden. Only once had the mask fallen off. Hopkin had been about to put on an Ellington record. 'Not that,' Bill had said, and his face was taut. 'If you don't mind. Too black. Not his skin, his gloom.' Laughter blurting out. Part of the bond between them from the start was their sense of the absurdity of everything; aspects of a madhouse world which they recognised spontaneously together and rejoiced in. 'Dancing on the graves,' they called it, and it gave them a stance, a point of view they liked to think was uniquely theirs. They were so much in accord in those days that they seemed twinned: Castor and Pollux, the heavenly twins.

Meeting at teacher training college, they were separated by their marriages and by teaching jobs in different parts of the country. Bill went down to the south, moved over to Wales and lived in isolated villages, developing a fear of some demon in himself which was malevolent and self-destructive, so he always said. He had a dread of inheriting his father's history of mental illness, his speechless violence, once ripping the doors from a cupboard when Bill was a child and walking out of the house, followed by his wife's screams of abuse. 'Don't come back, good riddance,' she yelled down the street after him.

Bill's wife left him and came back again. He had a child and felt trapped. At his various schools he began friendships and broke them off. He had a wild streak which the kids liked, not aware of his desperation. He was unpredictable, zany. He started an affair with one teacher and the guilt nearly killed him. Winters frightened him, so he fought them off by running and walking hard, but it was the ice in his heart he feared most. He was forced to see therapists, quarrelling bitterly with them. Falling ill with a series of psychosomatic ailments he became increasingly frustrated and began to paint in his spare time. For a long time this worked. Now he was at home permanently and was driving his wife mad with his dangerous moods and rages. Marie took jobs to make ends meet, and as a way of evading him now their children had left home.

Chapter Three

Hopkin told himself that when he paid his mother a visit he would swerve over to see Bill and Marie. They were living on the edge of the moors outside Tavistock. Until then he would write. For the moment he did neither.

He had crawled into his hideaway feeling almost a revulsion, a numb coldness. None of his surroundings mattered. Nothing touched him or meant anything. The idea of Kafka, with his haunted death's head looks, had always prevented him from reading his books. Now he was a Kafka man, collapsed and sickly, refusing to die and unfit to live. Cutting himself off like this was lunacy – any therapist or counsellor would have told him so.

Yet all he had done was obey a blind instinct which kept telling him to seek out the part of the universe which had been shorn off, lost to him. What for? What did nature matter? What did the old ancestors who once lived in the woods and fields mean to him? He got up these mornings and looked out at the dripping trees shrouded in gloom, hearing the wind rushing through cold twigs empty of all life, blackened by wet.

And yet little by little he was becoming accustomed to it all. Like it or not, it was his domain. He walked out to the wire fence beyond the conservatory and surveyed the pigs, only a dozen or so, rooting for grubs among the bushes and abandoned fruit trees at the edge of the wood. Once in a burst of warm sun at the every end of November the enormous sow lumbered out into the open from the sty and flopped on the mud, steam lifting off her flanks as if from an oven on legs. And he'd found that if you reached in and scratched a young pig under the ears or on the top of its head it sank down on the earth in an ecstasy like a cat.

He had begun each day by dreading the grey daybreak and the end of his oblivion. Staying in bed was worse, curled around his misery like a child, liable to be plagued by a succession of thoughts and memories the sum total of which was futility, the defeat of his attempt to go on.

And you had to go on, there was no help for it. He struggled not to drown in a sadness of waste. When, one despairing morning, he caught himself actually longing for death, for an end of this dreadful struggle to continue, he clambered out in a mad clawing rush. He stood trembling in the clammy cold bedroom, fists clenched. He was done for, done for. He groaned aloud. The chink-chink of a bird outside his window, sounding as feeble as his own state, made him shake his head in disgust in spite of himself.

Gradually, compared to the moment when he had touched bottom, it got better. The bathroom, a basic affair with damp patches up near the ceiling, was his first port of call. He emptied his bladder dolefully, doused his face with violent handfuls of icy water and descended to the cold kitchen. Up and dressed he began to gain a little courage. He boiled water in the kettle and took it upstairs for a shave, possessed suddenly by a craving to get rid of his bearded wild-man visage. Clipping near to the skin he was still left with a turfy stubble, a mask for hiding in. He imagined a new-born face, free of care like a baby's, rising to meet the sunrise. Clearing the thick stubble from his jaw and cheeks, scraping cautiously at his upper lip where he was always liable to nick himself in his clean-shaven days, he watched his naked face emerging with its expression of staring alarm. What did he fear? Not death. No, it was the mockery of a life without point. The awful shapelessness of modern life. That was what Lena redeemed for him, simply by being herself, by her unflinching realism. She was rooted in something beneath him, under his feet, deeper than him. Now he wavered about helplessly in every wind.

He got out his journal and made a note of his act, in an attempt to anchor himself, hoping the shave would turn out to be an act of grace. The trouble with a journal was this: you were never sure what it would make you say. Gradually, slowly, as he wrote, he began to feel better about himself.

He hoped he was not deceiving himself when he noted that the mornings, from being grisly, were becoming the little pools of utter quiet from which he ventured out on his day. He thought of himself as soiling, unless he took care, the pure gift of the morning. A long-submerged desire to attempt a poem stirred in him. 'Midnight to Morning Glory' he ought to call it, if he ever found the courage to try. He ate his bowl of cereal, sipped his hot tea and sat trying to catch the slightest sound. The silence that had once oppressed him he no longer minded.

Little by little he had begun to establish a routine for himself. At the sink he washed up the white cup and saucer, the blue bowl, the spoons, and stacked them to dry. He found the ritual comforting.

He thought he might join Stroud library and get out a book for the long dark evenings: anything would do. He would stir himself to write to his mother, to his son and daughter-in-law, to his friend Bill even. And there was Sally, his step-daughter. Then he could anticipate the postman, and letters coming.

Would he feel threatened? On the contrary he felt touched by a weird excitement at the idea of such contact. Surely there was nothing to fear from letters, slipping in quietly without prising him out of his isolation. He would still have control of things. It surprised him to realise that his lonely vigil was something to be guarded jealously.

Looking back, he saw himself as suffering the first wretched weeks and somehow staying intact – though he thought he was mangled beyond repair – and now he had started to value some gain that he couldn't describe. He thought in terms of a prize, a gift that was being bestowed on him by the silence itself, or by the unspeaking presences surrounding him. He had been forced to listen and they were now telling him things. Secrets. But what nonsense that was! All the same he reached for his journal and noted it, for what it was worth. Another day he might understand it.

It dawned on him that his journal was his daily work. Curious to think that a man was lost without some task confronting him. And he did feel a certain trickle of satisfaction in his veins after he had communed with it – if that was the word. Matisse, he had read somewhere, had regarded drawing as a kind of meditation. So were his journal entries if they were anything: mixed with the grit of facts, daily happenings, birds, animals, the weather.

Mainly though he saw them as letters addressed to his dead wife. Especially that was so if he wrote in the journal late at night, the emotional time of the day. He would feel tears shaking his heart, his hand. If she could only speak to him. He longed for answers to questions. Had she called out a warning to him, seconds before the crash? He couldn't be sure, and the uncertainty tormented him. It would be so characteristic of her, for she couldn't bear them to hit anything. He remembered her distress when they had once struck a pheasant. Coming back the same way a few hours later she had made him stop the car. They got out to search for the bird but there was no sign. Was this the spot? Had it lain stunned and then revived? She consoled herself with the possibility. 'It's going to get shot anyway,' he told her, driving on.

'I don't care. It was alive. I shall hate myself if I've injured it.'

'You haven't. I might have done.'

'Same thing.'

'Show me the bird and I'll start grieving,' he said, irritated at last.

Morning journal entries were different. They were his work. Whatever stops you working becomes your work, someone said – Camus? Hopkin was conscious now of the clay of words, trying to ease out of the mud of his sentences something living, searching for the spring of freshness, wanting some living water to bubble clear. When he stopped, gave up, he was limp with effort, understanding that he had indeed been labouring to reach a hidden source of – what? Did he want to write poems again?

All his working life, sporadically when a teacher and more ambitiously when a lecturer in the polytechnic at Bristol, he had written poetry. He had even published a little, in literary magazines and small presses. Teaching the great poets in the English department had undermined him, and then his students, when he had creative writing sessions to teach, wearied him with their self-pity and their dreary experimentalism. At least the love-lorn among them were genuinely moved. But their pulpy words were no easier to take, and threw doubt on his own. Mostly his colleagues were a jaded lot, parading a concern for literature they had long ago stopped feeling. Did he feel it? Not if he told the truth. It was never literature, it was the spark of life jumping into him from certain writers. And how rare that was.

Finally he resigned. He had a reduced pension, and to eke it out he went back to chalk-face teaching, taking on supply work. He lacked the knack for giving a performance and would feel exposed as a fraud, keeping order by leaking out aspects of himself he most despised: intolerance, and the menace of his suppressed rage. On that night of the accident he was telling his wife how he felt, driving back from a visit to his mother.

'Give it up, then,' she said.

'Just like that?'

'If it's what you want.'

'But is it?'

'So you say.'

'That's only what I don't want,' he said, feeling immovable and stupid like his late father.

They went on in silence. 'What are you really saying?' she asked.

'I wish I knew,' he said, and laughed.

She sounded out of patience when she spoke again. 'When you do, let me know,' she said.

'Don't be angry.'

'I'm tired,' she said.

He glanced at her. Her unsmiling profile, though he admired it, was no encouragement. 'If you were me, what would you do?' he said.

She thought for a moment, then said, 'I'd ask myself what I really wanted.'

'I'm nearly sixty. My life's going down the drain.'

'Make a decision then.'

'I've met this woman,' he joked, badly.

'That's what you need,' she said, 'someone who understands you.'

'Oh, you understand me all right. That's what's so hard.'

'What would you like to do every day?'

'Write poems that nobody wants.'

'Then do it.'

'I might find there's nothing there.'

She didn't speak again. And now she never would.

Chapter Four

He got into the habit of sitting still in the mornings, resisting the temptation to shoulder his rucksack and go tramping down the road towards the town – he thought of it as a large village – ostensibly for his bits of shopping but really for the bustle of people and the buzz of traffic. He kept that, usually, for the afternoons. When he gave in and spent more time there he accused himself of waste.

In the mornings he worked at his journal and then simply sat in a trance, not even thinking. The slow movement of time washed to and fro in the kitchen where he had settled, and he drifted with it. It was curious, pleasant. Idleness was an art: he thought of Whitman. He wasn't aware of the world outside his windows unless a van or a car disturbed him, chugging past on its way to buy organic beef at the big house. That happened rarely. Finally he got up, shook himself and stretched, rousing himself with a mug of coffee. It was the nearest he had ever come to another way of life, out of the grind of the world. He imagined the trees of the wood standing out there in the dead of winter, part of the stillness as he was, in abeyance like him.

He was beginning to explore now, toiling up the steep field beyond his front windows to where the sheep gathered under the bare oaks. He couldn't get very near them. They saw or smelled him coming and moved off nervously. He tried circling them with pretended indifference, gradually moving in closer. It didn't work. Once Michael Symonds hailed him, chugging along one of the rutted tracks in the Land Rover, bales of fodder in the back for the sheep. He got in beside him. It was nearly dark. The headlights picked out eyes shining everywhere like glow-worms. Hopkin couldn't believe it: there were dozens.

'Rabbits?'

'The fields up here are swarming with them. Now, where are those sheep?'

He nosed over the brow of one rise and there they were below, a tight knot of them clustered against the stone wall near a gate. No problem now in getting close. The truck pulled up and the animals gathered round eagerly. A big ram was butting the side of the vehicle with rhythmic blows, rocking it on its springs, impatient for the fodder. These sheep, only a dozen, were almost pets. They all had names. The real income of the farm, Hopkin understood, came from its cattle. The Symonds family were united in their humane treatment of beasts. He wasn't surprised to learn that the cows and bullocks had names too.

He had been a few times into the wood, but not far in. One blowy morning he pulled on his gum boots, his duffle coat and a cap, impelled by a desire to go so far in that he was lost. There were few paths and it was easy to lose your way, in a maze where everything looked the same, where you lost touch with the sky. The split logs he kept burning on his open fire in the evenings came from in here. He had stopped stoking the cumbersome great boiler, deciding to wait for the severe cold he expected later. And lighting it each morning was a curse, and he'd never managed to keep it in all night. You began with paper and kindling in the mouth of the cylinder, then the smoke billowed and stung your eyes as you tried coaxing it into a bigger blaze. Once well alight it was a devourer, insatiable. He found it satisfying at first to take the wheelbarrow round to the mountain of timber and return with a full load, but always the thought of the boiler's raging hunger nagged at him. Did it need stoking again? Was it going out? He gave up on it, contenting himself with a fire in the living room hearth at night. In the kitchen he could switch on a space heater.

He walked down the drive away from the farm, as far as the first track to the left through the coarse grass and tangled briars. This led straight into the wood, sloping down to an area of boggy ground that sucked and clung to his boots. To get beyond this he had to haul himself over a fence. The top rail was rotten and let out a crack, but he was over.

As if a voice whispered in his ear, he looked upward before the wood swallowed him, as if taking leave of the sky. The gusty wind tore at the low cloud, and he saw a scurrying sun running out into clear holes before being buried again. Earlier there had been showers of rain. He wondered what it might be like as a filtered rain came down, standing in the mysterious dim light of the wood.

He went in deeper. Suddenly it seemed enormous, stretching away secretly on all sides. He guessed there must be wide ridings where they took the tractor and trailer to load up the felled and split timber, but here there was nothing. No paths, no horizons, no directions to anywhere. It shamed him to think he knew so little about trees, when here he was stumbling about in their kingdom. It was so easy to imagine the early men dreaming up a religion of trees. He could at least tell the big grey oaks from the beeches, the birches by their pale puce bark, gleaming queerly in the wood's permanent twilight. In the distance he could make out a dense plantation of young firs. He went past a hazel copse, hanging out its lambs-tails.

For all the mud on the roads and in the fields, here on the floor of the wood it was quite dry, almost dusty. He went crunching over it, over dead sticks and the remains of bracken. Suddenly he was in a space; he could hear water tinkling, and at first couldn't trace it. Then by a low bank he found the spring, welling out minutely on to the moss and pebbles and leaking down the slope past a clump of elder bushes. Further in still, he started climbing upwards, keeping upright with difficulty on the ridges and outcrops of rock. Panting, he sat down on a tree stump. Then, in the hush and secrecy, totally alone, he heard the rain whispering down, making its subtle, soothing sounds. The wind blew stronger and he listened to that, far up over his head, the trees responding with their soughings, active at the tops, their perfectly straight trunks immovable.

He discovered at last the wide riding he had expected. There was the felled timber, the sawdust, a pile of logs ready for splitting. An old abandoned tractor stood rusting, up to the axles in undergrowth and half swallowed by brambles. Then he was out in broad daylight, unable at first to get his bearings, feeling a pang of disappointment at being back in civilisation again.

He was at the edge of a field. Beyond was the road, Stroud one way,

Ash the other. Three cows were grazing, Guernseys, though Michael had told him that the grass lacked nourishment now. Standing guard over them was the creamy bull, Pedro, curls plastered on its broad brow by the wet.

Chapter Five

He was in the bakery one day buying a loaf when the red-bearded stranger from the *Golden Hind* spoke to him.

'How's things?' he said.

Hopkin didn't recognise him, except for a fleeting memory to which he failed to put a face. He felt idiotic.

'I'm all right,' he said, vague and confused.

'You don't remember me, do you,' the man persisted. 'In the pub.'

'The *Golden Hind*!' Hopkin said. 'I'm getting senile.'

They were moving out of the shop together. 'Probably it's this,' the man said, and touched his half-grown beard.

'Julian, is that it?'

'Well done.'

Hopkin felt exonerated, pleased with himself. 'Be seeing you,' he said at the next corner.

'Care for a coffee?' Julian asked. Saying this he hunched down in his anorak a little, as if prepared for a rejection.

Hopkin, startled, found himself answering, 'Why not?'

'I live just up the road. My old banger's round here.' He led the way up a side street to a white van covered in mud and grime. 'Looks disgusting but it goes.'

Inside it was squalid, water swilling underfoot. They set off, spluttering and coughing. 'Clapped out, it is,' Julian laughed. 'Like me.'

Hopkin glanced sideways at him. 'You look fit enough.'

'Appearances aren't everything.'

'True.'

In no time they were driving past the entrance to the Symonds farm. 'That's where I'm living,' Hopkin said.

'I know. Everybody knows everything round here.'

'So I'm told.'

'A formidable man, Symonds. Doesn't pull his punches.'

'I agree. He's impressive but scary.'

'Single-minded people can be like that.'

They drove on. Passing a splendid house behind a high Cotswold stone wall, rampant lions on its gateposts, Hopkin exclaimed at its beauty.

'Ashcome House. Where the brigadier lived. He's dead now. Famous in his day.'

'What was his name?'

The driver jerked round his head. 'The same as mine. He was my father.'

'It's your home, then?'

'My mother's, not mine. I prefer where I am. Up a lane in a caravan. We're nearly there.'

'You're the black sheep,' Hopkin joked.

'I'm a remittance man.'

'I know the expression. What does it mean exactly?'

Julian laughed his rare, funny yap of a laugh. 'They pay me to stay away.'

'Why, I wonder.'

'A long story. They find me disruptive, that's about it.'

'Who's they?'

'My mother and sister. She's the one, my sister, who finds me really objectionable.' He laughed again, a sour yapping noise. 'To tell the truth I'd be worried if she didn't.'

They turned right and sank down steeply into the rainy village of Ash, deserted in its ancient mouldering charm except for one old man, straightening up by his front garden wall, trowel in hand, to glare after them suspiciously. Climbing again past affluent converted barns and detached stone houses they ascended sharply between high banks and the trunks of young ash. A field gate stood open and they passed through. The caravan stood against the thorn hedge. Birds flew up.

'You live here alone?' Hopkin asked.

Julian was unlocking his caravan door. 'Unless I can entice anyone to stay, yes,' he said over his shoulder. 'Not easy. Mod cons are essential these days if you want a partner.'

Stepping up and in, the visitor was surprised to be met by a fug that wrapped him round. He saw the slow combustion stove near the window, the stove pipe through the roof. He had been glad to escape the dirty litter and loose grit moving under his feet and was expecting more of the same here. On the contrary it was a shipshape interior, neat and inviting. Check curtains at the windows hung crisply. He wondered if a woman's hand had been at work here recently.

'I could ask you the same,' Julian said. He had lit a butane gas ring and was boiling a kettle.

'Yes, I'm alone.'

He was puzzled by the other's accent, not working-class exactly. Maybe a touch of Australian. Had he been living out there? What did it matter – except that his remark about the brigadier father put him in a class he should have instantly recognised, as you always do in England. Julian's speech seemed to belong nowhere, except perhaps as a repudiation of the education he must have once had. He had once met a famous poet's son, an ex-public schoolboy who sounded broad Cockney. Julian's speech verged on the uncouth, but seemed worked-at. And there was that unmistakable confidence of the well-to-do.

'How d'you like your coffee?'

'White thanks. No sugar.'

The two men eyed each other, in one of those pauses meant for sizing up. It was a moment for floundering, and instinct: no chance of any real communication. All the same, Hopkin appreciated the idea of inviting fate, of letting things happen now and then. And at least with a stranger you could imagine something different. He sipped his coffee and glanced curiously at the other man, who had sunk into an almost apathetic silence as if discouraged. Maybe, having made the gesture, extended his hand so to speak, he now thought better of it. 'What does he want of me anyway?' Hopkin thought. What was this invitation about?

As if reading his thoughts the man said, sounding crudely direct, 'How does it suit you, then?' He stared down moodily at the floor.

'The coffee? Fine.'

Out came the queer barking laugh that had no humour in it. 'I meant the life.'

'I don't get you.'

'Living on your own. Is it what you want? Does it suit you?'

Hopkin was being confronted. He stared into the blue unblinking eyes of the other man. 'I'll tell you later,' he said, 'when I've done more of it.'

He had answered without showing, he hoped, that he intended to resist this too personal approach. Some trust needed to be established, and he felt none.

Julian came to life and was suddenly a charmer, his smile flickering, even his voice changing its tone to an altogether more sympathetic register. 'Forgive me, old man,' he said, leaning forward on the upholstered bench. 'You mustn't think I'm poking my nose in.'

Hopkin was recalling the sardonic words of a fellow lecturer, telling him once that you could get away with murder if you smiled. 'Poke away,' he said. 'I don't have to answer.'

'That's right, you don't.' Julian was nodding emphatically. He pondered a moment. 'We're free agents. We don't have to do a damn thing we don't want to do, that's right.'

Both men sat quietly in what Hopkin felt was a strained, slightly embarrassed silence. He blamed the other man for forcing this intimacy on him, probing too soon. He cleared his throat. 'What was his name, your brigadier father?' he asked, and then laughed. 'Sorry, I mean your name.'

'McShane.'

'Irish?'

'Yes, I suppose. Or Scottish. If you go back far enough. Sounds absurd but I've never bothered to find out.'

Hopkin took the plunge and said, 'What about you? Does your single life suit you?'

'Ah well. Let me put it this way.' He seemed to warm to the subject, eager to be expansive suddenly. 'I'm here by choice, but I'm not alone by choice. I'm separated. My wife left me.'

Hopkin nodded, sympathetically he hoped, though wondering if it was the wife who deserved sympathy. 'So we're a couple of loners,' he said.

'You're separated?'

'Permanently. I'm a widower.'

There was no response, no gesture of false sympathy, for which Hopkin felt gratitude. The men eyed each other in the cramped, cosy space that kept forcing them together, against their better judgement, Hopkin thought. Then suddenly he stopped caring. All his life he had lived warily and where had it got him? Here he sat in a field with a total stranger, and what did they have in common? Only their singleness. It struck him that they were typical of the times, not knowing exactly what he meant. Rootless, both of them. Julian was younger, in his mid forties probably, but was in the same boat, belonged to the same fragmented male species as himself. He saw them as a sorry pair and he wanted to laugh. Instead of being depressed by the thought, what he felt was a rush of elation. Struggling with his desolate insides, sitting in a caravan he'd never seen before, wishing a woman was on hand to counteract the bleak atmosphere generated by two men adrift, it made him want to laugh. He didn't understand a thing; he was sick of trying to understand. Let the ship roll, he remembered an old acquaintance saying once to Lena when she was fretting over her daughter's future. One is never utterly alone after all.

Again the younger man acted as though reading him. He stirred on the bench impatiently, picked up a booklet that was stapled into a mustard yellow cover and handed it over without a word. He cocked his eye at Hopkin as if desirous of something, wanting a sign.

'What's this?'

'You can take it with you,' Julian said, his smile secretive.

Hopkin disliked the presumption. The man could be crass, disdainful. Was he being over-touchy? His first instinct was always, whether he minded what he was asked or not, to do what was wanted of him. Deep inside he was barricading himself from intrusion and cursing whatever had driven him to it. Outwardly mild-mannered, he held his tongue, while underneath his obstinacy stiffened.

'What is it?' he asked again, fingering the booklet.

'Take it.'

Hopkin handed it back without opening the thing. 'Why don't you tell me about it?'

The man shrugged. His smile had turned to slow ridicule. 'It's not mine. It was passed over to me yesterday. I nearly threw it in the bin. Then last night after I got into bed I read it through. God, I thought, what's this grubby effort about? Values and Vision, it said. What's that? I had the same reaction as you. Turns out it's the manifesto of a group of twelve people, hammered out in London last year. So what, you might say. Not another bloody group.'

'Twelve does sound familiar.'

Julian jerked up his head and smiled his subtle smile, and his face, that looked rather haggard and embittered in repose, flowered sweetly. 'Yes, right,' he said. 'Only this time no messiah.'

'Go on, I'm interested.'

'Well, what struck me was the scope, the sweep of it. True, it's much better on what's wrong than on what if anything can be done. About the alternative to the present shitheap it's as vague as smoke. Community politics, I ask you! Does anybody now if they're honest like their neighbour enough to get together for the common good? I doubt it. The vision part seems to advocate a whole crop of tiny groups like the one that produced this, hundreds and thousands of them, joining up across the country in a kind of network. That seems pie in the sky to me.'

Hopkin said he was inclined to agree, though he wished he didn't. 'Is that it?'

'You'll have to take it away with you. I can get another, but I don't need to. I get the picture. Strikes me as deadly accurate so far as it goes. Sees exactly what's happening now, on all fronts, and how it can only get worse. What's your opinion of that?'

Hopkin, shifting uneasily, said yes, he thought the Jehovah Witnesses were right about one thing, we were going to hell.

His new friend or whatever he was didn't laugh. He talked on, faster, as if he wanted to overwhelm his listener. 'Take that horrible subject, work, and how it gets to be so detestable, such a necessary evil for so many people. Yet when you do something for love, you jump out of prison at one go.'

'Arbeit macht frei.'

'Which means?'

'Work makes freedom. Over the gates of Auschwitz of all places.'

Julian ignored this. Excited, in the grip of his passion, he waved his hands. 'Take one of the examples they give here: the Recession. Unemployment is built into the system. One evil breeds another. Change the rules and the values, they keep saying here. How, though? They point to the vast era of great empires that's come to an end – Russia the last – and we rush on as if nothing has changed. The implications are immense. We're so up to our necks in the dead past, the arms trade, delusions of grandeur, panaceas of science, that we're like sleepwalkers. We're halt and blind. America, if we did but know it, is crumbling, on its last legs. So is organised religion. Who knows what to believe any more?'

He handed back the booklet.

Hopkin accepted, though with reservations. 'This is the answer?'

'It's one answer,' Julian barked. 'See what you make of it. My heart started to sink, I must admit, when I read about the call for these clusters of little groups. We have to stop protesting, and find out what we are *for*, it says. Does anybody care enough? Has it gone too far? Are we all acting out a giant death-wish? More to the point, do I like people enough? Or myself, come to that? If I don't, why care about anything?'

Hopkin got to his feet. 'I'll read it and see. Thanks.'

'Hang on, I'll run you back.'

'No, I'd like to walk, thanks all the same. I've been promising myself a walk in this direction. It's beautiful up here.'

'It's not bad,' Julian said indifferently. When he switched off, he looked around vacantly, not interested. Somehow he couldn't seem to look outside himself.

Pocketing the booklet, Hopkin glanced at the abbreviation, SUMIGE, 'a Small Unstructured Multipurpose Independent Group of Equals', and he let out a groan.

'What's up?'

'SUMIGE. Sounds like a cross between sludge and sewage.'

Julian laughed. 'All the same, bear with them. People-power, that's the thing. Don't you believe in that?'

'Once I thought I did.'

'This shambles,' Julian prophesied hoarsely, as though relishing the thought, 'is going to fall to bits of its own volition one day. Then it's people-power or nothing.'

Hopkin was making for the gate out of the field, followed by his new friend who stuck to his heels like a shadow. Irritated, he said over his shoulder, hearing the impatience in his voice, 'I thought you didn't like people?' Out in the open he was feeling dazed, ineffectual in his wavering scepticism but not caring, and it came to him that all he wanted truly was to be alone again, free to be himself.

'I don't! I don't!' he heard Julian shouting. His raucous yapping laugh shattered the gloomy afternoon.

Chapter Six

Another day. He had gone dreaming past noon. The conservatory door was the only entrance for visitors, should he ever have any. Someone was knocking at it. The front door was permanently locked, sealed up he imagined, disappearing under a thick veil of honeysuckle.

It was the cowman, Donald. He spoke shyly, but looked levelly at him with his cat-green eyes. Hopkin was struck by his grave, sad demeanour. He was an educated man. Unlike Symonds, he had no trace of a country accent.

'Phone call for Mr Hopkin,' he said quietly. 'Up at the house.'

'That's me,' Hopkin said. 'I'll be right there.'

The man nodded and clumped away, cumbersome in his caked boots.

Hopkin stood in the farm kitchen. The phone was on the dresser. It was his son, saying, 'I didn't know what to do, whether to call you or not.'

'What's the matter?'

'Colin's in hospital.'

'You mean an accident?'

'No, no. They suspect meningitis.'

'God, no.'

'They're not sure yet.'

'I'll come, shall I?'

'Dad, there's nothing you can do.'

'I'll come.'

'I only rang to let you know.'

'I was thinking of coming anyway. Hilary won't mind?'

'Good God, no. This is your place.'

'See you soon.'

'I've got to go now,' Paul said, and Hopkin heard his daughter-in-law in the background, calling something.

'I can hear Hilary.'

'Yes, did you want a word?'

'No, give her my love. I'll see you both soon.'

Henry Symonds had come into the kitchen. Hopkin stood against the dresser with the phone still in his hand, looking lost.

'Excuse me,' Symonds said stiffly. 'I thought you'd finished. We should have the phone in a different place, I've been saying so for years.'

'I've finished, thanks,' Hopkin said. 'Sorry to have bothered you.'

'Like a cup of tea?'

'No, I must get on. Thanks all the same.'

'Please sit down a moment.'

Hopkin ignored him. 'It's my grandson,' he said, and he could hear his voice, too high and gabbling. 'In hospital, they're not sure what it is. They're only in Cheltenham. I'll go and find out what it is, what's the matter – I'll go straight away I think.'

'Leave everything up there, don't worry,' the big stooping man said. 'We'll lock up and so on. You go and get ready, if you've decided that is.'

'Yes I have, I'm going.'

'By train?'

'Yes.'

'Michael's somewhere nearby. He'll take you to the station.'

'No, please. Can you ring for a taxi?'

'You go and get ready,' Symonds said. 'Do as you're told, man. It'll be one or the other.'

'Right.'

'Get off, then. We'll see you in due course, Mr Hopkin.'

As the train approached Cheltenham he felt a clutching sensation in his gut and knew he was afraid. He was afraid of another death. He was afraid of his flat, of whether he would be able to bear it there. Don't let there be another death, he prayed. Anything but that.

He left the train and the rather shabby deserted station and began to walk blindly through the streets he knew so well. It was too soon:

he hadn't expected to be thrown back among the cruelly familiar surroundings so soon. What had happened, what could be the matter? Colin was such a sturdy little lad.

The streets and buildings of this bustling town, elegant though they were in this district, with avenues of trees and fine proportions to the tall old houses, streets and squares of white houses, had mysteriously changed character and become hateful to him. So had the people, hurrying past with shut faces. It was all coldly indifferent, windows glassily staring, the doors glossy with coldness. The damp day enveloped him. Had he ever liked it, if he told the truth? He reasoned that it was the contrast with the countryside he was now embedded in which made it so hard to take. Yet when he had first moved to live on the farm he had felt alien and unwanted, the very fields and trees resisting him, or so it seemed. Now he wondered how he could have ever lived in this town. Everything spoke to him with an air of complacency, of insufferable selfishness. It looked superior, as if it saw itself as the centre of the universe. Cars chased each other's rear lights and pulled into the entrances of wide, important-looking gravel drives.

But of course inwardly he knew why the town hadn't mattered, how it had been refashioned and made part of his world in those early days. The slow invasion that was marriage, the contentment as his body and spirit knitted together was something he had known here in the long years with Lena, locked away with her and his son and step-daughter at the top of the house out of reach of everyone, growing invisibly in a kind of counterpoint, so he liked to think, to the children's urgent physical growth. The word maturation would come into his head, a relic of his college days. 'I want you to be kind to yourself,' Lena told him gently. She taught him how.

There was no refuge for him now in these houses. The very doors rejected him – they were right to shut him out. He had no place here now. He had never truly belonged, and now he was a traitor in the camp. His own flat with his son and daughter-in-law in it existed in a different part of his consciousness, separate from everything else. They and it were bound up with his dead wife, lifted out of this cold indifference, existing in a kind of bubble.

He reached Eagleton Square and turned in. He felt deplorably weak, forcing himself to take strides he was afraid to take, his face strained and white. He would know the worst in a moment.

He went up the broad, cracked steps to the wide portico of the communal porch. He could have knelt down and counted the cracks, certain he would have known the number, as certainly as he knew the number of the years of his marriage. The door stood open as always. The stairs rose before him, cold and disregarded, the linoleum cracked as it had always been, shabbier than he remembered but still in one piece, the glossy paint of the stairwell yellowed and ugly where the light caught it from the bare bulb at the turn of the stairs.

He went up in the dead hush, through this neutral, uncared-for territory that the tenants on the three floors had long ago stopped noticing, as he had. He reached the top landing and stood a moment outside his own door like an intruder, listening to nothing. There was no stir of life. He had thought his retreat in the depths of the country was silent, and so it was, but with a bristling silence that charged the air. This silence he found deathly, as if life had withdrawn from it. And he imagined a stale dust descending on him, burying him where he stood.

He had his key, but for some reason rang the bell. After all, it was no longer his home.

Paul opened the door, his face agitated, tense. 'Dad, you must have jumped on the first train. You needn't have done that.'

Hopkin followed his son down the long corridor, aware, now he was a stranger, of its abrupt change of direction, and then the release from the windowless gloom into the light of the inner hall. Even at twilight there was still illumination from outside. For all his anxiety he looked upwards at the source, to a skylight he had completely forgotten. 'I wanted to,' he said to his son's back.

In the pleasant square sitting room with its high sash windows, the frames flaking, he asked for the latest news.

'Sit down, Dad. You look terrible. I'll make a cup of tea.'

'No, really, I'm okay. When did it happen?'

'Two days ago. Let's see – this is the third.'

'Where's Hilary?'

'She's in the hospital. They let mothers sleep there when a child's in danger. She's in a room close by.' He rubbed his forehead distractedly, a gesture his father knew well, and went on to say rapidly that the news this morning was much better. 'They've moved him out of intensive care – it's not meningitis after all. The symptoms were similar – vomiting, temperature, headaches, flashing lights in the eyes – those are gone now, thank God. Some kind of virus they can't identify.'

Hopkin nodded. He sat awkwardly on the plump new sofa. The gas fire with its imitation coals burned cheerily. The walk from the station at speed meant that he was insufferably hot. He passed a hand over his face. He began to drag his sweater over his head, his arms weak.

'I'll turn this down,' Paul said. 'He's aware of my every move,' thought Hopkin, touched and uncomfortable. His son jumped up and twisted at the control hidden under the cast iron grill. 'How about a cup of tea?'

'Yes, go on,' his father said.

Left alone, he wanted to cry out. Lena was everywhere in this room. 'It's a different carpet,' he thought wildly, in an effort to distract himself. When Paul returned with the loaded tray his father looked across at him frantically.

'You sure you're all right?'

Hopkin, staring at his son, noticing afresh how quick and nervous he was, with his slight build and his clever, rather flinching mouth – which would turn down contemptuously or look vulnerable with his mood – could only nod dumbly, not trusting himself to speak. In this awful room he was afraid he might not be able to keep his voice steady. He could feel the churning of tears in his chest, behind his eyes.

'I must say you don't look it.'

'It's this room,' he said.

'What? Oh yes, of course, stupid of me.'

'What about you?' he managed to drag out.

'Oh not so bad considering.' He gave a short laugh to express his disgust. 'If one thing hits you, depend on it there's another waiting round the corner. They've just made me redundant.' He was a rep for a firm selling office equipment. 'Ordinarily I'd have been really down. One thing about this scare with Colin, it's put everything into perspective. What the hell, eh?'

'I'm sorry, Paul.'

'Don't be. Hilary's taking it worse than me. Be sorry for her, not me. And now this.'

'She's not coping?'

'When we took Colin in she was so distraught I thought she was breaking down. But once she decided something in herself, and then found she could stay there with him, that was the turning point for her. She'll be back to normal soon, now Colin's out of danger.'

'Good. That's good.'

Hopkin sat thinking that he and Hilary had never hit if off, for reasons that were still obscure to him. She was cool, contained. His views irritated her. He had this image of her twitching angrily at her skirt when he spoke out sometimes – was it something about his tone she always disliked? He had always found her brittle, falsely affectionate with Colin in front of him and Lena. He would tell himself it was nothing, she would change, relax, life would rub the sharp corners off in time. Lena, he'd sensed, had a certain antipathy too, but when he'd pressed her she had been reluctant to own up to it. She was wiser, perhaps. If nothing was going to change, make the best of it.

When he heard the key in the door and she came in, her overnight bag in one hand and holding little Colin by the other, he stood up impulsively, delighted. The moment she saw him, a shadow went over her face. It was fleeting but he saw it. So it was the same, no change. She couldn't help herself. Well, neither could he.

Paul had leapt to his feet. Not knowing whether to be glad or angry, he just gaped at his wife. 'Why on earth didn't you let me know?' he asked, almost petulant. He went over and kissed Hilary, kissed the boy. 'Why didn't you let me come and fetch you?' he moaned.

'I didn't have a chance,' Hilary said. She was fair, bright-cheeked, with small sharp features and keen, pretty eyes. 'Somebody whisked me off in a car – I thought they were putting me in an ambulance, putting us both in, and I thought how silly, Colin's as right as rain again thank God. There was this nice lady sitting in her car – a voluntary helper it said, the sticker on her windscreen. I didn't even ask who she was. Rude of me, wasn't it?'

The crisis over, she was clearly flushed with triumph and relief. She kept pulling the little boy to her, who stood docilely staring at his grandfather.

'Granpa's here, Colin,' Paul said. 'He's come specially to see you, haven't you Granpa?'

'I certainly have,' Granpa said. He held his arms out wide.

'Aren't you going to say hello?' Paul urged.

'Of course he is, when he's ready,' Hopkin said, smiling at the boy, glad to find he still could.

Suddenly the little boy decided. 'Hello Granpa,' he cried, and ran to the man leaning forward, who opened his arms again.

'Ah, there's a boy,' he said, grateful beyond measure. He hugged the tiny figure. Tears pricked his eyes. 'What a time you've had, Hilary,' he said over the boy's head. 'You've come through with flying colours by the sound of things.'

'I've had the fright of my life,' she said tartly. 'We both have.'

'And they don't know what it was?'

'Not certain, no. A viral infection of some kind.'

'A mystery then.'

'Quite.'

'They're all a mystery to me. You're a mystery,' Hopkin said to the boy. 'What are you?'

'A mystery,' the boy said.

'That's it, you've got it. Aren't you clever!'

'I'll make coffee,' Paul said. 'We've had a cup of tea.'

'I don't want one,' Hilary said, a statement you didn't argue with. 'I'm dying for a bath, that's what I'd like. Is the water hot?'

'Yes, there's plenty.'

'Wonder of wonders.'

She hung uncertainly in the doorway. Her hair was cut in a close shape around her head. Hopkin had forgotten how small her mouth was. He had to twist round to speak to her, aware that she was unhappy about him being here, not sure how long he would stay. She had come rushing in with her news, her triumph, and here he was stuck in the way, spoiling it. He was guessing, and perhaps he was wrong. He genuinely felt that she had a point, that he was unfit to associate with people. But what was it about her that he could never deal with? It might have been simply that he made her nervous. But he didn't convince himself.

'I'll be off soon,' he told her. 'I only came to see for myself how things were, and find out if there was anything I could do.'

'Stay for the night at least – now you're here,' she said, too quickly, with what Hopkin guessed was a false expression on her face. She went pink. 'Now you're here' had sounded like an accusation. She rushed on, 'You can sleep in Marianne's room if you like. We still call it that, though we hardly see her. It's Colin's, really. Or you can test our new sofa bed.'

'I'll do that.'

'It was good of you to come.' She had never addressed him by name. If 'Dad' stuck in her throat, Matthew would have been acceptable. Evidently it was beyond her. Strange, he thought, how reduced you are somehow without a name. He had tried more than once not to feel resentful, and always failed.

'I had to find out, that's all,' he said. 'It couldn't have come at a worse time for you either.'

'How d'you mean?' she said sharply.

'Paul told me his bad news.'

'Yes, that.' She was looking past him at her husband, her eyes jumping, as if to say. 'You haven't wasted much time.'

'Don't let me keep you from that bath,' Hopkin said. It came out stiffly, and he sighed.

'I can't wait,' she said, going.

He felt immediately less tense with her out of the room. He thought guiltily, 'Apart from anything else, we're just ridiculously shy of each other.'

He looked around, at all the details he remembered. He could imagine Lena coming in. Paul sat mutely with his arms around the little boy, who was subdued, no doubt because of his experience, but also feeling the need to be on his best behaviour with his grandfather in the room. He was a bright, sensitive little lad, already with his father's looks.

'Tell me how things are with you, Dad,' Paul said. They had always been able to talk openly with each other. Now he looked his father in the eye. 'What are you up to, living like a hermit?'

'I'm no hermit,' Hopkin said. He tried to laugh. 'That's to say, whatever I am at the moment, I wouldn't recommend it as a way to live.'

'You mean for others?'

'Or me either.'

'Then why do it?'

'Good question.'

'Which you're not going to answer. You're hardly in the thick of things, are you?'

'For the time being, no I'm not.'

'But it suits you.'

'For the moment. If "suit" is the word.'

'Then what?'

He thought a moment. 'I haven't thought about afterwards. Not yet.' He stopped, while his son waited patiently, knowing he would go on. 'It's a different existence from anything I've known before. At first I didn't see how I could stick it. The loneliness, the silence. I'm still working myself into it, liking it, if that's the word, a little more each day. And myself into the bargain. That's the hard part, I find. Liking yourself.'

'Now look, it wasn't your fault that Mum died. You know that, don't you?'

'I survived. That takes some living with. Don't you think so?'

'Dad, I can't imagine what it must be like.'

'And you never blame me? In your heart?'

The young man looked shocked. 'Of course not, no. Never.'

Though he had warned himself not to, and now hesitated, Hopkin found himself saying, 'Hilary?'

'What?'

'Doesn't she have doubts? Blame me?'

'No, why should she?' Paul said stoutly. His father didn't quite believe him, but left it there. Nothing would alter his loss. The grief that kept knotting in his chest would remain.

Then something came free inside him, and he smiled. 'It's good to see you again. Are you happy here in the flat?'

'Yes, very. Until the job collapsed, that is. The firm's on the rocks, so I hear. But if you want to come back and live here again you must say, we'll find somewhere, no problem. I've got my redundancy money, and Hilary's still working at the nursing home. We'll be all right.'

Hopkin shook his head. When he spoke again it was out of a moroseness that had crept back to gather round his heart. 'I can't see myself coming back here, ever,' he said.

Feeling he might make a fool of himself he stood up, went to the window and looked down on the gravel access road, the iron railings, the dense tangle of shrubs and the area of private park beyond. Nothing stirred. A car buzzed past occasionally, visible in the gaps. It was all exactly as he remembered it. Pain everywhere.

'I can,' his son said.

Again his father shook his head. 'No. Only as a ghost. Which is what I am. Talking to other ghosts.'

Hilary made up the sofa bed and he thanked her gruffly. He lay there for a long time before getting up at last to turn off the light. As his eyes became accustomed to the darkness it gradually lightened. The glow from the street lamps penetrated the curtains. He could see across the room. As he fell asleep he was telling himself it was still the same day, and he heard again the cowman, Donald, knocking on the side door, and saw himself hurrying out to reach the phone.

Next morning he escaped as quickly and decently as he could, marching away down the wide pavements under avenues of chestnuts that were bony and stark, blackened now by the late October rain. He made his way to the station. He had been glad to see Paul, shifting about under Hilary's sharp gaze as he always did. His bright spark of a grandson, fully recovered as if he had never been ill, had put a rare smile on his face. The child's skin was so soft and fresh, his spurts of energy making him run over the stuffy room like clear spring water. You could see the joy in the working of his chubby little legs as he went tumbling forward.

Now Hopkin was out in the blowy, friendless spaces of the town he no longer liked, not caring that no one knew who he was. He shrank particularly from people who cared about him. He preferred indifference. He was going home, but to a shelter rather than a real home. Lena wouldn't be there waiting, or anywhere. He wouldn't see her again. Lena was dead. He said it in his mind, his lips moving as he walked in the streets they had walked through together: Lena is dead. He walked on blindly with nowhere to go.

On the train he got a seat in the corner of a half empty carriage against the window and stared out at the landscape bathed in morning light. It had been suffocatingly warm for him in the flat, too cosy, too intimate, not to his taste. The small stone house waiting somewhere ahead, standing damply against the trees with its bare rooms, not even an armchair worth the name, the stone hearth stained up to the mantel with woodsmoke, it would greet him indifferently when he reached it, slipping in to make a fire. The austerity suited him. Anything was better than the stifling domesticity of a hearth where he no longer belonged. His pleasures were the meagre, essential ones to do with keeping warm, staying alive and no questions asked. It could be seen as cheerless: there was no love in it, no one cared what he did, and his mood darkened and lightened with the sky. When he tussled with entries in his journal he began with the weather. He wondered if he was experiencing a weird change, an unknowing. He used to be a regular newspaper reader. Now he choked on newsprint. Opinions were especially abhorrent to him. Anything which got between him and the immediate world he could see, touch and smell was to be avoided. The rest could go on regardless of him. He was thankful to be ignored, left with the world he breathed. He thought he might be learning to live all over again.

PART TWO

A MISSING LIFE

Chapter Seven

As October became November – he had lost track of the date, and often had no idea of the time – he was enticed out one afternoon by the sun in a clear blue sky. He thought vaguely he would try to intercept the route of the Cotswold Way and walk along in the direction of its end. This marked public path started at Chipping Camden and wandered over the wolds as far as Bath. It stretched for nearly a hundred miles, said the booklet he had bought and then forgotten about. The thought of the thousands of ramblers who marched along it purposefully all through the year put him off, though the winter would have thinned them out, he thought.

He wouldn't go far along it. He had passed the signpost on the road a time or two, pointing up a hill by the side of a long twisty drystone wall. He ought to try it and see.

Instead, his spirits lifting as he stepped into the pale sunlight and heard the pigs foraging, the air sharp on his face and ears, he allowed his boots to decide. They took him into the depths of the farm, past the cow barns and the tractor with its trailer of dried hay, past the handsome old farmhouse, looking big enough in this light to be a mansion, then on by the pool ruffling its surface under the stiff breeze, water lapping against the clumps of rushes.

Up ahead, not far, was the house on the hill that he'd been curious about ever since Symonds had told him the story. He had lived there once himself as a boy, he mentioned casually to Hopkin. Now it belonged to a South African millionaire the farmer evidently loathed. He was hardly ever in residence. The only ground was the area of gardens around the house, and he had sought to extend his land by adding on to it the farm which was Symonds' whole reason for living. Every so often he increased his offer.

'The man's crass,' Symonds had said. 'I find it hard to be civil to someone I can't stomach. I say I'm not interested and a few weeks later he's back again, smiling like a fool at my door. There's no dealing with such a creature.' He added with a snap, 'He's got dogs up there when he's at home.'

Then he's damned, Hopkin thought. He asked mildly how the South African had made his money.

'How does anybody? I've got no time for millionaires.'

'How about socialist millionaires?'

The socialist farmer shrugged, then took Hopkin's breath away by saying blithely, 'At least that way they justify their existence.'

From where Hopkin now stood, short-sighted though he was, he could see the yellow of the hired machinery. Symonds had mentioned alterations and extensions going on, and excavation for a swimming pool. Standing by his own pool, which had been dug, he said, for herons and water-fowl rather than himself, he told his tenant what he thought of this prime example of millionaire's folly.

Over to the right Hopkin spotted a herd of bullocks. 'I'll work my way round there from the house,' he thought. Had he spoken aloud? These days he had endless conversations with himself, now and then with Lena. It might not be long before he was talking to himself on a regular basis. 'Like a nut,' he told himself grimly. When he was alone, what did it matter? As though he had stumbled on something important, he made a mental note for his journal to the effect that a human being can't exist without company. If you had no fellow humans to talk to, you invented company. That was what talking to yourself was all about.

The banality of his thought amused him, or it might have been the blowy sunshine that was making the world brighter, and him with it. His dark blue duffle coat, bought in an Oxfam shop, hung on him from the shoulders like a loose shaggy pelt.

He had an impulse, halfway up the steep shale of the track, to squat down on the grass and rest. It was too wet, so he kept on. He was working his way up a hill, conscious of its shape, of the huge rhythmic folds of earth and rock rearing and crouching around and below him. A painter of landscapes would have wanted to swing his brush in these rhythms, to know the land by copying these massive contours.

A low-flying aircraft, military, with swept-back wings, tore into the sky from nowhere. It exploded with violence over his head, with a terrifying ripping rage as if he was its target, assailing him before he could do anything. He clapped his hands to his ears. 'Bastards!' he yelled after it, long after it had gone exploding over fields and valleys in the direction of Birmingham. He had an image of the sky in shreds, fluttering to the ground in bloody ribbons.

He climbed on, shaken and sick. The house which had looked small when he had started towards it, now looked impressive. He could see no sign of life. An ornamental stone parapet ran around the eaves. The roof was so shallow, it looked flat. He was nearing a gate and a wire fence which he understood was the boundary of the Symonds farm in this direction. Beyond was a copse of hazels, mixed with silver maple. As he got closer, birds burst into the air and settled again. The sun flaring in the bright blue sky, a blue of such delicacy, gave him a craving for spring.

The yellow digger lifted the arm of its steel shovel above the low wall running around the property. Its claws shone. The other side of the house must be a top road where they had access, he thought. He saw why the owner kept pressing Symonds to sell. He would even have settled for half the farm, the farmer said in disgust. 'Which shows how ignorant he is about farming. I just about survive on what I've got.'

He had reached the end of the boundary wall, moving right to the high pasture in the distance where the herd of cattle grazed, when a man came round a corner of some outhouses and called out. The wind blew harder up here, and whatever he said was immediately snatched from his lips. Hopkin stopped and waited. He was aware of the loud thumping of his heart, brought on by the stiff climb or something else, a tension, a fear. The man approached the wall. 'You,' he said. Too young to be a caretaker. Maybe a construction worker, about to start up the digger. He was wearing a brown boiler-suit.

Hopkin identified his fear: it was his mother's animal fear of strangers, that made her want to bolt and hide. Hopkin found himself thinking with sudden longing of the rowan, laden with berries when he came, growing so sturdily in front of the place he now called home. He thought of it now as a friend. Solitude was a clean state.

'Hey, you,' the workman bawled. 'Where d'you come from?'

Hopkin stopped still. 'Who wants to know?'

'You from round here?' the man persisted, suspicious but more conciliatory.

'Down there,' Hopkin said, pointing back the way he had come.

'Visitor, then,' the man said.

'I live there. Why, what's the problem. Am I trespassing or what?'

'You might be,' the man said. He narrowed his eyes significantly. Hopkin went on walking.

'You aren't the owner, I take it?' he called back.

The man turned away. 'They've had break-ins here.'

Hopkin ignored him and carried on. He was on a high field that was all ridges and lumps, so high that he felt he was flying. The rough ground made it difficult to walk away with dignity. The sunshine rapidly restored his spirits and he walked along, balanced on the shelving uneven turf, thinking, 'This is best, away from people.' He thought he felt a prickling between his shoulder blades and swung round. The man up on the terrace was still there, staring. He was being seen off. The surge of misanthropy in him blotted out the sun. He felt cut off, apart from humanity. 'And why not?' he thought savagely. Why bother with people? Let them keep away from him, and he from them. For the first time, dark-soaked, he felt he had been born solitary. Long may he stay so.

But if only Lena could see all this, he told himself, moving on along the rim of the little bowl of farmland. He wanted nobody to approach him, he admitted his wife and no one else. He ached to share his mornings with her, so that the chill on his heart could go, so that his heart lived again. The view from up here was magnificent, the farmhouse below had shrunk and looked perfect, set down by the pool that was winking in the light. He made a vow to paint a word-picture in his journal for her. With every step he left his wretched, dismal feelings behind.

It had rained in the night and the grass was still wet. He came slowly nearer to the eight or nine bullocks and could see the figure of a young woman going to and fro among them. He hesitated; thought of veering off in another direction. The woman took no notice of him, and he was thankful. He went reluctantly forward. She went up to one beast and it stood submissively in thrall to her as she stroked its broad meek head. Hopkin noticed her fine intelligent profile. Drawing closer, he thought he must have been seen. If he had tried to touch the animal's head it would have shied away from him. The woman was being treated as a familiar, he supposed that was it.

Afflicted all at once by bashfulness, he made to swing wide and avoid her. He was startled, astonished to hear himself called by name. Whoever she was, they had talked to her about him.

'Beautiful day, Mr Hopkin,' she cried, freshly smiling.

'Not like November,' he said.

She was still pummelling the neck and shoulders of the passive animal, murmuring to it affectionately. 'Oh, I don't know,' she said warmly. 'I can remember some wonderful November days here.'

'There you have me. I've not lived here before.'

'How are you liking it?'

'More and more. Though it took some getting used to.'

She tossed her head, as the wind blew hair into her eyes. He saw now she was older than he had first thought. But he could give her twenty years.

'By the way, I'm the daughter,' she said, and laughed. 'The older one, that is. Helen.'

Then he knew. 'You're the doctor.'

'In Worcester. I'm the one that got away.' She cocked her head mischievously. 'I hope my father didn't sound too disapproving.'

'Not at all.'

'He's not keen on the medical profession.'

He considered her for a moment. She had turned away again to converse with the animal, treating it like a huge pet. Her strong jaw, her clear grey eyes and her forthright manner reminded him of her father. There was nothing coquettish about her. She was attractive, yet he felt he was talking to her man to man.

'He's not keen on the fellow up there either,' he said, pointing back at the South African's house.

'Oh, he's told you that?'

'You sound surprised.'

'Mr Hopkin, I'm not surprised by anything my father does. He's a law unto himself.'

'True.'

'Does that bother you at all?'

Hopkin thought, then shook his head. 'Bothered isn't the word. You know where you stand with him, like it or not. He comes out with things other people are afraid to say. He seems to be someone who decides the rights and wrongs of an issue by consulting his insides. If it makes him feel bad, it's rotten. I admire that. I only wish I could be more like it myself. I'm too eager to please, too afraid of not being liked I suppose. Your father gives some sort of lead, even here, even if nobody's heard of him.'

'He's more known than you think.'

'Excuse me, that's my ignorance.'

'A real fly in the ointment, you might say.'

'I've not met anybody quite like him,' Hopkin said sincerely.

The woman, still with her hand moving on the bullock's neck, said thoughtfully, 'Me neither.' She turned again to the big docile beast. 'I haven't met anyone like Aubrey either.' She turned to Hopkin playfully, without self-consciousness. 'This is Aubrey, by the way. Isn't he perfectly gorgeous? Doesn't he steal your heart? Wouldn't you say he puts us humans to shame?'

Hopkin was more than ready to agree.

'Look at those eyes!'

'You speak to him as if he understands you.'

Indignant, she cried out, 'Of course, of course he does! Every word. Of course. He's a most intelligent animal.'

'Do they all have names?'

'Every one. The pigs, too. Did you know that pigs were the most intelligent?'

'I'm learning all the time,' he said, smiling.

'It's true.'

'Compared to?'

She laughed. 'Don't tempt me. Compared to those who think they're dirty and stupid.'

He asked about cows, those shitty-arsed Herefords he'd seen down below.

'We don't have a dairy herd. They're just for ourselves, for milk and cheese. We farm beef.'

'What about slaughtering?'

She spoke firmly. 'One day there'll be slaughterhouses for organic farmers. But we accompany them, go all the way, make sure all's well. They have as good a life with us as we can give them, right to the end.'

He said he could already see that for himself, and was a convert to the Symonds creed. She was so unaffectedly warm and open that he risked a joke. 'I think I'll enroll in your practice, for some of the Symonds treatment.'

'I'm not a G.P. I'm a paediatrician.'

They laughed at that. As he moved away she called, 'I'm glad my father rented you the little house.'

He acknowledged her with his hand, his heart light with his moment of elation, his triumph of human contact, and began clambering down the hillside. Nevertheless he was happy to be alone again, making for the dwelling that was not his, where his ghost book, as he now called his journal, lay open and waiting on the kitchen table.

Once there, he gathered up a bundle of kindling and spread it on the hearth to dry, ready for his evening fire. There was no warmth in the place but his body glowed from his exercise. The silent enclosed space, after the wide blowy spaces of the open fields, suddenly touched him with its air of expectancy and its worn sticks of furniture. Like someone stumbling on a refuge for the first time he felt grateful for the walls, the roof. What must it feel like to be stripped of everything? He stood on the threadbare carpet before the hearth, then knelt down to clear the ashes from the grate. For a moment he was motionless. Someone coming upon him might have thought he was praying.

He thought he might read Thoreau, though he had never been drawn to him, and neither had Whitman. Going into the kitchen he recalled Thoreau saying that there was no need to feel lonely, since our planet belonged in the Milky Way. It didn't help, but the conceit made him smile.

The simple meal he prepared was something more, for once, than a means of staying alive. Realising this, he felt he was making progress of a kind, back to the land of the living. Since Lena had died he had eaten from necessity, without any pleasure. Sensuality never entered into it. Lena had taught him how to be good to himself, and the gift was lost with her. But this time, instead of joylessly stuffing a little food into himself he would take care over what he cooked.

He gave up on his recipe book, a dog-eared paperback for people of slender means who lived in bedsitters, and began making a soup that he hoped would be as nourishing as a stew. He sliced onions and added oil to the bottom of the saucepan and heated the onions slowly, watching them turn yellow, then yellowy brown as they lost their crispness and became slithery and soft. He boiled water and made stock with a chicken cube in a beaker. Then he set to work slicing and chopping everything in sight, everything he could lay his hands on. The stock bubbled and he turned it down to simmer. Celery, carrot, parsnip, potato, a can of sweetcorn, tomato, it all went in. He added salt and black pepper, and sprinkled in mixed herbs, brought it back to the boil, then to simmer again.

Encouraged by this basic meal, which tasted reasonable when he helped it down with granary bread and a glass of stout – though next time he would make a proper stew, with enough lamb or beef to give it a tang – he made a cheese and potato pie the next day, toasting it under the grill and serving it up with a can of baked beans. He felt pride: he had stopped eating just to live. The change had come of itself.

What other changes were at work invisibly, inside himself? And then he thought, forking his hot meal into his mouth, that since the death of his wife he had not once dreamt of her. He had longed for her to visit him in sleep. Why were his dreams cluttered with blurred sequences and broken shards meaning nothing to him, while Lena stayed away? He felt his strength draining away as a black heaviness clouded his heart, and put down his fork. He sat weakly crying. Then the spasm of intolerable loss passed from him, leaving him weak as a child. Here he was sunk in nature, lost, like a babe in the wood. Lost, lost. He turned back to his meal, but his pleasure in it was gone. He swallowed it down somehow, with repugnance.

Chapter Eight

Often these days he wished he was like his mother, with her blind faith and her simple girlhood religion. If he could have prayed, it would have been to ask for courage. When his spirit sank low in him it was because he had lost courage. Then he consoled himself by thinking that perhaps his journal entries were a kind of praying, an expression of thankfulness. For what? At times he felt anything but thankful, such as the day when he asked in a rage where she had gone, how could she have abandoned him. Wasn't it John Clare who had gone on writing letters to his wife for twenty years after she was dead? But he was in the asylum, mad. Perhaps madness was the heart's refusal to accept unbearable loss.

He wrote at last to his mother. The letter said:

> Dear Mum, I hope you got my note saying I am perfectly all right, warm and confortable and taking care of myself. I would have written a proper letter before now but I kept telling myself I would be coming to see you. It is just that all my energy at the moment is going into making this place into a sort of home. I don't mean with alterations, it's not mine to do that. I never felt less like altering anything.
>
> Mother, you have never really ever spoken to me about Lena and what you feel, felt about her – not even whether you liked her or not. There is no law which says you have to like someone who is in effect a total stranger. Did you like her? Were there things you disliked or which irritated you about her? Did you feel loved by her at all? And what about my father? I should love to know. The great fear the grieving person has is that the loved one will grow dim in the memory and little by little slip out of it, until one day there's nothing left to hang on to. So you see I would be grateful for anything at all. Photographs are a cruel deception. There is the image of the lost face, caught for one frozen moment, at which you stare madly, then when you try to go behind it there is nothing, a black hole. It is just a piece of flat card.

As he wrote, it dawned on him that all he wanted to do was write about Lena. He should have asked about her well-being, and whether she was warm and comfortable as he said he was. He brought his letter to an end as decently as he could.

> Shall I come and spend Christmas with you? If I don't see you before, that is. Take care of yourself and keep nice and warm, won't you. Does your young friend Janie from across the road still keep an eye on you? When are you due for your next cataract operation?
> Forgive me for not phoning. I can't do it, not yet. But you are on my mind every day.
>
> Your loving son,
Matthew.

A few days later there came a letter from Bill Walsh that alarmed him profoundly. His oldest friend said he would come and see him. Hopkin seized at once on the phraseology: he didn't *want* to come, was the implication, but he would. Close to paranoia suddenly, he read the words as a dark threat. No, he cried to himself. His hand shook. There was no way he could have someone, anyone, here. He'd come here to be alone, his mind gabbled. And Bill was frequently desperate. The very thought of Bill's desperation, blackening the frail peace he had fashioned for himself, drove him into panic. How could he forestall him? Why couldn't he be left alone by everybody?

He reprimanded himself bitterly. To believe that his friend had threatened coldly to come was a commentary on himself. But it was no easier, worse somehow, if he saw the message as a gesture of love. He had come here to leave everything. He had listened to a voice telling him to go away, to leave all he knew. In the abiding silence of this place he had even begun to learn how to be still, and more remarkably, how to escape himself, get outside himself. The trees stood patiently, stoical as he would like to be, waiting for him to become aware of them as presences outside himself. The birds in the wood were silenced by the approach of winter. On frosty nights he had gone and stood outside, standing like a post against the fence separating him from the abandoned orchard, where the pigs rooted during the daylight. At night they disappeared into the sty. He had seen them lying there, pressed up together contentedly, fearing nothing, and the great sow with her oven heat like a capsized tree trunk. He had gone to hear the owl. Nothing. Why did its tender cry, throbbing like the voice of the night, sounding so close and intimate, thrill him?

When he was calmer he sat down to write to Bill. And he thought of Marianne, his stepdaughter. He ought to send her a word: they had always hit it off. The fact that she would never bother to reply was beside the point. Her natural father had washed his hands of her: he was the replacement.

He wrote:

> Dear Bill,
>
> I have your letter. It was good of you to write. In spite of all the letters we have written to each other over the years your handwriting on the envelope came as a surprise, a shock even. Who could have given you my address? Was it Paul? I only ask because I feel bad about not telling it you myself. The reason I didn't is to do with this place, and what I am trying to do here in solitude. It's the hardest thing I have ever tried to do.
>
> Please don't feel angry or rejected when I say that I'd rather you didn't visit me here. I am doing a balancing act and may fall off at any moment. It's a day-to-day thing. Next week or the week after I may want to see you very much.
>
> How would you feel about my coming to see you and Marie there in Devon after I've been to stay with my mother? I'm going there for Christmas possibly. I could come either before that or in the New Year. Tell me what I should do.
>
> If I write more my pen will carry me away. Our friendship is no longer what it was, and maybe we've left it too late to rebuild the splendid thing we once had, which I gloried in and thought would last for ever. Maybe what we will have in the future will be different, more realistic. Kill the ideal, we used to tell each other, but we never did it. We loved each other and maybe that's enough.
>
> Enough of our golden youth. Writing this is almost like having you in the room with me. It's the next best thing. Bear with me, and don't come yet, please. I have a little routine now. In the mornings I try to write in a log or journal. The morning is the sober time of day. In the long dark evenings I sit by my fire, watching it burn down, keeping it going. I might write a letter as I'm doing now, or listen to some music, if I can find something cool and clear, with few instruments, not big thumping apocalyptic stuff that shakes the foundations, the kind we used to like. My foundations have been shaken enough. The evening is when emotions are liable to spill over messily, so excuse the emotionalism of this. And let me hear from you soon, properly.
>
> Your old friend in spite of all,
> - Matt.

Chapter Nine

Hopkin's sister June had invited their mother to spend Christmas with her and her family in Dorchester. He had received a note from his sister telling him this. He would be welcome too of course, she said, her words cautious as ever. They got on, after a fashion, though she had never approved of something in him that she sensed but was unable to name. He couldn't see himself going.

He packed his rucksack and set off to visit his mother. There had been a succession of hoar frosts. Surfaces were treacherous. The wood he was leaving behind, the hedgerows and the rough grass of the pastures were coated with frost as if in preparation for the not-too-distant festivities. Every bramble, each twig, each thorn, even fence wires and blades of grass carried their separate upholstery. Going away was like leaving a wonderland. The atmosphere as the day advanced was thick with mist, settling down over the land like the drifting of smoke.

The train journey was tedious but he sat in a trance. The whole of England was under frost. He stared and stared until his eyes ached at this world bled of colour. In a field close to the train he saw a fox break cover. He felt his heart jump as it ran, and he marvelled at its heavy dark brush. It put a spell on him. When it vanished he was so moved, so full of surprise and regret that he wanted to weep. He knew then that the glue holding him together could so easily fail him.

All the way down to the southwest he was thinking of Bill, of what their eventual meeting might be like. It had been nearly three years. Lena had grown hostile to him gradually, though without ever admitting it. She would be sardonic when a letter came. 'Here's a letter from your Bill.'

'Why mine?'

'Well, he's hardly mine. I doubt if he ever notices me.'

'That's ridiculous – of course he does.'

She wrinkled her brow. 'Some women get between their husbands and any man he may have been friends with in the past. Am I that sort of woman?'

'Ask yourself.'

'Stop being evasive. Am I?'

'I've never thought so.'

'If you did, you wouldn't tell me.'

'I can tell you honestly that I don't see you like that.'

'How do you see me?'

He sighed. She was discontented with her appearance, groaning exaggeratedly in disgust when she caught sight of herself in the mirror. Her need for reassurance had never been greater than now, when she mourned the loss of her young looks.

'Whatever I say, you won't believe me,' he told her.

'You look better than me.'

'How better?'

'Younger.'

'I don't feel it.'

The question of Bill came back. 'When you two get your heads together,' she said resentfully, 'I may as well not be here.'

'That's because it's an odd number. If Marie came, wouldn't that be better?'

'It would if she spoke. She sits down wide-eyed and hardly says a word.'

'What do you want her to say?'

'Anything. She's like these girls who keep their mouths shut because they think it makes them mysterious.'

'She's hardly a girl.'

'She's not a mystery either.'

'She doesn't say much because she's frightened of you,' he said, tongue-in-cheek. He knew it wasn't true.

'Not that one.'

'What then?'

'How would I know? She's bored, probably. All the kindred-spirit stuff you two go in for.'

'According to Bill, she finds it hard to put her thoughts into words. She finds words difficult. That's why she's a potter.'

As time went on, and Bill twisted and turned in the sprung trap of himself, he would break away from home occasionally and come alone, or with his little girl, to see them. Often he came unannounced. It infuriated Lena to open the door and find him standing there, his smile twisting self-consciously as he tried lamely to ingratiate himself with her.

'Why couldn't he have warned us?' she would fume afterwards, torn between her fury at his lack of consideration, his bland assumption of a welcome, and her guilt at treating him so coldly.

'It was just a spur of the moment thing I expect,' Hopkin would say in his friend's defence. 'He's in a state, you know that. Have pity on the poor devil. He can't leave and he can't stay.'

If that was true of Bill Walsh's home life, it was true also of his visits. No sooner had he been there a few hours than he was chafing to be off, back to Marie. He rarely stayed overnight. The truth was that Marie was the centre of his existence. He almost hated her for it, but it was so.

Then gradually the devil that had taken root in him came between the two friends. Hopkin saw that behind Bill's smile, which had once delighted him, lurked a malevolence. It wasn't aimed at him, but at anyone not caught in the trap of self-loathing and mad self-consciousness like him, worn out with endlessly watching himself. Schizophrenically vivacious in company, he gave way at home to bitter outbursts, after which he sat in a corner and refused to speak. The chronic insomnia which afflicted him later was some years off. He dreamt of communal living as a solution to his problems, but was powerless to act. He read in order to accuse and punish himself, immersing himself in the horrors of death camps. One such indictment by a survivor led him to write to Primo Levi, who replied in Italian, 'I salute you in your effort to become better.' Convinced that isolation was the cause of his and all our ills he announced that he was working on a socio-philosophical book which he would call, he said, 'The Need for Others'. He told Hopkin once, quoting Levi, 'It is only in nothing that we can become something.' His friend nodded, moved and half understanding, only too aware of the anguish behind the words.

Bill's suffering was all too visible to Hopkin but he felt powerless to help. He sensed the danger of openly sympathising, sensing he would have been hated for it. Or was he making excuses for himself? What Bill craved was for someone to attack him, lash him. He lived for Marie's accusations, which he did his best to provoke, since they came so rarely. 'You're so bloody calm,' he jeered, 'so forgiving. Saint Marie, you are.' She put up with him endlessly, bore his moods and his malice in silence, or with little words of comfort like a mother. The attempts to love him only added to the pain of being himself.

Rarely now there came flashes of the old Bill. Where had their seizures of infectious laughter gone? Hopkin would be touched, standing at a bus stop, by the husky voice saying goodbye to him. The old glory days, revelling in the mere joy of being alive in each other's company, ran back again for an instant. Hopkin felt bereft. He saw the mute appeal in his friend's eyes and turned away with a full heart as the coach carried him off, shamed by the relief he felt at seeing him go.

The familiar fields of his mother's Dorset countryside stirred him as always, the train bringing him home, the unchanged gaunt little country station coming near slowly, like a dream. The train slowed and halted. He shouldered his rucksack and climbed down. Should he walk into the market town and get a bus, or take the short cut across the fields? He got as far as the stile, unsure as about everything else in his life, and climbed over anyway. This was home to him, yet he had lived in Birmingham till he was twelve. It was home because his mother was here. He tramped down a cow track and then came to barbed wire, ducked under and started to climb. The modern brick farmhouse, isolated on the crest of the hill, looked deserted: but then it always did. A sheepdog ran out. Hopkin stiffened, pretending unconcern: he had a fear of dogs. The dog glanced at him and then squatted down against a wall.

He went scrambling down across ground given over to thistles, all mounds and ridges. He came to a stream and the wooden footbridge. To get over he had to negotiate a quagmire, churned up by cattle. Now he was in the stream valley bottom, on land too rough and steeply tilted to farm, a wild spot, overrun with rabbits, that his mother had loved when she was mobile. She called it 'Happy Valley' and would go there at sunset to sit on a bank that would be studded with primroses in spring. She liked the peace, she said, and listening to the silvery calling of birds, the liquid songs of blackbirds. She had joined an art class at the Women's Institute, and came out to her secret domain with a sketch pad and some crayons. She sketched the blue tits on her bird table in the patch of front garden outside her cottage window, colouring the primitive shapes of her bird-bodies with touches of gouache. To Hopkin the strangely askew perspective and the clumsy bird shapes were moving, alive even, in a way he couldn't have explained. The life of a thing didn't come from accuracy, or from the brain, but from somewhere else.

His mother was expecting him, but he hadn't been sure what time he would start out. He went down past the allotments and between thorn hedges to a steel farm gate, then he was at the rear of his mother's cottage. If he went in through the converted outhouse at the back he might frighten her, he thought. So he walked around past the end cottage in the short row and rang the doorbell. Strange, it was, standing in the gloom of winter, how his heart beat louder as he stood on the threshold, taking note of every detail.

The world, stretching away on all sides, seemed to have gone to sleep. No one about. In the suspended quiet he noticed the paint peeling on the door. He ought to attend to it while he was here. There was a brass lizard door-knocker, superseded now by a loud electric bell because his mother was very deaf. Because of her age, his sister, who lived twenty miles away, came over most days in her car to see that she was all right. Dorothy Hopkin was a stubbornly independent woman, though increasingly infirm. One of her dreads was the thought of being a nuisance to others. She was determined to stay in her own home as long as she could. Her daughter saw to her comfort, fetched her pills when she ran out of them, cooked her a dinner whenever she came, played cards with her.

His mother opened the door and then retreated. She always did this. It wrenched his heart to see her, glad though he was to be home and welcome, able to do no wrong, the beloved son. How stiffly, painfully she moved; stiff as a board she was with rheumatism, yet not bent. How ancient she looked.

'Come in, dear,' she cried. 'Let me have a look at you.'

'That's my line,' he said loudly. 'I've come to look you over. How are you, Mum?'

'Old,' she said, pulling down her mouth.

He put his arms round her, unable to say more. What a bundle of bones. He kissed her old cheek, then brushed her dry lips with his.

'So am I,' he said. 'Anything we don't know about? What about your eyes?'

'Oh, the one they did is wonderful.'

'That's good. Will they see to the other?'

'Yes, but for cataracts they have to wait six months between one and the other,' she said. 'Don't ask me why.'

'Right, I won't,' he mumbled, forgetting, half to himself.

'I can't hear. What did you say?'

'I said I won't.'

'Won't what?'

He threw up his arms, waved his hands, laughed. 'Never mind!' he shouted.

'I'm not that deaf,' she grumbled, and made her way into the kitchen, a narrow cave-like space, with great care, her legs and whole body encased in stiffness, holding on to the edge of the door, the counters. Hopkin knew better than to help her.

'Where are you off to? What are you going to do now?' he asked, and she swung round to face him.

'I'm going to make you a cup of tea,' she said. 'Or would you rather have coffee?'

To his surprise she had heard with her back turned, though it was much easier when they were face to face. 'Whichever's easier,' he said.

'What kind of answer's that?' she said. Yet it was what he always said, and so her reply was always the same.

In the evening they sat on either side of the electric coal-effect fire, with its flickering orange light underneath to provide a glow. Sometimes, she told him, she switched on the orange glow alone, when it wasn't too cold that is.

'To economise, is that what you mean?'

'No, to cheer myself up. It's more cheerful.'

'But it's not real,' he laughed. 'There's only a coloured bulb in there.'

'It's more cheerful,' she said stubbornly.

They sat opposite each other in the wing chairs occupied by his mother and father for as long as he could remember. Somehow they got on to the subject of food, of meals he'd enjoyed when he was a boy.

'You liked smoked haddock,' she told him. 'We had smoked haddock on Fridays. Remember that?'

Of course he did. And going up to the market with her on Fridays to exchange his *Hotspurs* and *Skippers* for old magazines and comics he didn't have, at a stall where you could swop them for a small sum. 'How did that happen?' he asked her, wanting to know. 'Wasn't I at school?'

'It was the summer holidays I expect.'

'I suppose so.'

'Would you like smoked haddock tomorrow? You will be here tomorrow?'

'Yes, I'll be here.'

'Would you like that?'

'It's Thursday tomorrow, not Friday.'

'I know it is. D'you think I don't know what day it is? The man with the fresh fish comes round in his van on Thursdays.'

'Right.'

They talked some more about food in the old days because he could see it pleased her that he remembered. 'I loved apple fritters,' he said.

'And treacle pudding,' she cried. 'Wasn't that your favourite?'

'I thought it was spotted dick.'

'Was it?'

'I'm not sure. I liked it, anyway.'

'It might have been,' his mother said. She smiled at him and went on, 'What shall I make you tomorrow?'

'Whatever's simpler,' he said, laughing. She shook her head in mock disgust.

Later she told him he looked well and he pretended to be offended. 'Why shouldn't I be?' he demanded.

'Living in that godforsaken place,' she said, 'with no one to look after you.'

'Look after me? I'm sixty years of age.'

'Men are hopeless at looking after themselves properly.'

'So you like to think.'

She wanted to know how long he intended to stay holed up there. 'It's not natural.'

'What isn't?'

'Not seeing anybody for weeks at a time.'

'I can see whoever I like. I went to see Paul and Hilary and Colin. I'm here seeing you. When I go I shall call on Bill perhaps.'

'I like Bill,' she said. She hadn't seen him for at least twenty years. 'How is he?'

'Not very happy.'

She was lost in her reminiscence and didn't heed his words. 'When he used to come round to the house to call on you he was always nice to me.'

'That's a long time ago.'

'He said silly things, cracked jokes. He used to call me a barmpot.'

'Why did he?' her son asked. He knew perfectly well why.

'I'd tell him he was talking rubbish, and he just laughed, and I called him a barmpot.'

'And he said, "It takes one to know one, Mrs Hopkin".'

'Was that it?'

'I think so.'

'He was always nice, with nice manners. He was interested in me. He liked to sit in our front room and hear music on our radiogram, then when he left he'd come into the back and wish me goodnight.'

'He was fond of you.'

She sat back and looked at her son.

'Now what are you looking at?' he asked gently.

'You,' she said. 'Every time I look at you I think of your father. I wish I didn't but I do.'

He said lightly, 'Was he hopeless at looking after himself?'

'What d'you mean? He had me.'

'I'm joking.'

'He'd been in the army,' she said vaguely.

'So he'd have been all right?'

She snorted indignantly. 'No, hopeless. He'd have gone to pieces. I'm glad it wasn't him who was left.'

'I can't think of him living on without you,' her son said, unable to help himself.

Deep now in her remembrances, she said, 'He did have somebody else, once. In the war. When he was an air raid warden.'

Hopkin couldn't believe his ears. 'Are you sure?'

'Of course I'm sure. Marion her name was. Maureen. Something like that.'

'Was she someone he knew at work?'

'At the warden's post – I told you. They used to play table tennis together while they were on duty. Hours and hours they played.'

'What did you do?'

'He was a good man, your father. She got hold of him, that's all.'

'What did you do about it?'

'Oh, I threw a fit.' Hopkin stared, in his memory an hysterical scene stirring. 'That was the only time in our married life he threatened to hit me. He raised his hand.'

'But he didn't do it.'

'You know how big he was – a foot taller than me. He'd gone through the first war, seen terrible things, but he was afraid to hit me.'

'Afraid?'

'Of course he was afraid! He was in the wrong, you see. That made him a coward.'

'Are you saying it was the woman's fault, that she led him on?'

She looked at her son. 'Men are children when it comes to women,' she said.

Later still, about to go to bed, she turned and wept in his arms, saying the talk about his father had upset her. 'I don't want you to think bad things about him. He was a gentle, innocent man.'

'I know what you meant to each other, don't worry.'

'After he raised his hand to me, he cried.'

'And when his mother died. I remember that.'

'Do you?'

'I was sixteen. It gave me a shock.'

'That's right.'

'He didn't make any sound but I knew he was crying.'

'How?'

'He put his hands over his face.'

His mother was silent, on the stair about to go up to bed. 'He was a good father.'

'Yes,' Hopkin said, thinking to himself that he had hardly known that remote, private man. How he would like the chance to talk to him now!

'This is what I miss most,' his mother said. 'Oh, I do miss him.'

'I know.'

'All I want is to be with him again.'

'Don't cry.'

'I'm not crying. Goodnight, Matthew. Have you got everything you want?'

'Everything.'

'Are you sure?'

'Go to bed,' he said.

'I hate this part.'

'Goodnight, Mum.'

He feared her pathos, feared that he might stay and become a child again. Even with her back turned she knew what he was thinking.

'You'll be going tomorrow, will you?'

'Or the day after,' he said.

Chapter Ten

When it came to it he couldn't face Bill in Devon. Some instinct told him not to go, not yet. Was it instinct, he asked himself, or funk? He put a postcard in the mail making his excuses.

Instead he made for Exeter, to call on his stepdaughter. The thought of her put a smile on his face. Marianne had been a wild teenager but had blossomed as a young woman, determined to stay unmarried at present and forging a career for herself in local radio. She had invited Hopkin to stay several times since the death of her mother. 'Come any time, don't bother to arrange anything,' she had scribbled on the reverse of a card showing Bacon's *Screaming Pope*. 'I'm always here. Or if not I shan't be far away. Or Cressida will be here, she'll entertain you.' Cressida was her house-sharing friend.

He got there late in the murky afternoon, climbing uphill from St David's Station in a cold mist creeping out of the trees and bushes of the villas and the little park on the hill. The daylight was nearly gone, and the sharp incline made him short of breath. Cars swished past with their lights shining. On the streets at this hour, and in a strange town, everyone going home, was a bleak experience for him.

He ought to have phoned, he thought. He disliked phones now more than ever. If no one was at home he'd walk on in the direction of the prison, where there was a road full of bed-and-breakfast signs. This he did know about the town. In his twenty-six years of married life, this was the road of his one miserable act of infidelity. He was not cut out for it, as he soon discovered. The girl, unhappy as himself, in a marriage as rocky as his was stable, thought she wanted a strong father-figure, experienced, wise. Trying to live up to this he immediately regressed, out of guilt or loneliness, missed his home terribly and after a few days got her to take him back there, a father turned into a child. How they ended up in that Exeter road was as confused as their abortive affair. He liked to say afterwards, when they were friends, that the car – her car – was responsible; a joke she didn't appreciate. Seeing his plight she put her own misery aside and shamed him with a maturity beyond her years.

Marianne lived in a neatly designed modern house, very small but cheap to run. There was an area at the front with prickly shrubs and crazy paving, then the front door under a wooden canopy, opening straight into the one and only sitting room. Beyond that, a kitchen with enough space for table and chairs. Stairs rose out of the sitting room to a landing just wide enough to stand on.

Cressida was a teacher. A pile of exercise books for marking stood in a wobbly column on the desk under the stairs. She and Hopkin had met briefly before. She was dark, small. Her eyes darted nervously about. 'Marianne shouldn't be long,' she said, friendly but unsure. 'Can I get you some tea or something?'

He said yes, finding it pleasant to be looked after. He was on familiar ground with her work. She taught English, as he once did, though now he found it hard to believe. When she brought the tray of tea he urged her to go on with her marking. 'I know how it can pile up.'

'No, I'm glad of an excuse to stop.'

'I'd feel dishonest when I did marking – skipping all the time, giving up on the illegible handwriting. Unlike other subjects you have to read most of it. I'd end up making a wild guess.'

'Don't remind me.' Smiling.

'Having to make so-called helpful comments would find me out. I was a lousy teacher.'

'Oh, I'm sure not.'

'Oh yes. Mainly because I couldn't perform. Being an actor-*manqué* helps.'

'An actor what?'

'Somebody who fancies he could have been on the stage.'

'I thought I'd be an actress once. Till I joined an amateur company and found I was rotten at it. So I was a dogsbody instead.'

'Now you're acting for dear life in front of a captive audience.'

She laughed. 'I suppose.'

'I didn't inspire fear either,' he went on. 'Another strike against me. Never once did I feel really in charge. Every day was like walking through a minefield. When I first started I'd be so exhausted, I'd feel like crawling home on my hands and knees.'

'But who does feel in charge?' she asked, shrugging off what to her was clearly an irrelevance.

'It must be worse now than in my day.'

'You live with it. Don't let it bug you, I suppose.'

'So what's the worst thing you have to face?'

She thought for a moment. Laughed. 'Like you were, I get so awfully tired! It builds up. By the time I reach Friday I feel old before my time. At weekends I just want to sleep and sleep.'

'How about your colleagues?'

'We're all in the same boat. Drooping over our Nescafé in the staff room.'

'Shame.'

'Every now and then it's all worthwhile, though,' the girl added, suddenly grave and emphatic, refusing to give too black a picture.

Hopkin, ever conscious of his bereft state, asked neutrally about her boyfriend and how things stood. She was aware that he knew the story so far, from Marianne. It was no secret. He felt flattered when she confided that the warfare went on. 'With lulls, of course.'

'Like school,' he joked.

They laughed together.

'His name's Sam, is that right?'

She nodded, suddenly burst into life, fluttered her hands in the air. 'Still him. Been Sam for six years now, though that's amazing. We get on so badly sometimes that I wonder what on earth we're doing together. Then when we break up and the dust settles we ask ourselves what that was all about. Well, I do. Before you know it we're on the trapeze again. I suppose it must mean something, six years.'

She told him this so openly, with an almost childish innocence, that he was at first admiring; then felt his age. It was all subterranean in his young days, obscured, secret. Better or worse, it was different now.

'But you see eye to eye on most things?'

'Oh sure, it's not that. He seems to speak the same language as me but in fact he doesn't. We don't have the same agenda, that's the top and bottom of it.'

'Isn't that the same as saying he's male and you're female? Or can't one say that any more?'

He expected to be demolished, but she looked wide-eyed at him, comely and receptive, so that he wondered himself what he had said. 'You mean that's your experience?' she asked.

'Well, at the time, while it was happening, I did my best to adjust to it. But you have to admit, our satisfactions are fundamentally at odds with one another sometimes.'

'You can say that again,' she agreed comically, and he laughed again, surprised and pleased to find he could still laugh spontaneously. 'Why, though,' she asked in all seriousness. 'Whose fault is it?'

'It's how we're made, surely,' was all he could come up with.

They were beginning to subside into awkward silences when Cressida jumped to her feet and said at the window, 'Here's Marianne now. I though I heard her car.' Hopkin had been on the point of going out on a limb, suggesting that it was a matter of feeling good about oneself, keeping your self-respect, whether at work or with a partner. As Marianne came banging in exuberantly he was left wondering what the open-hearted girl's response would have been. These were questions he was asking of himself, of course. They would have come out more confidently than he felt.

He jumped up and submitted to his step-daughter's no-holds-barred embrace. It always left him abashed.

'Are you all right, Matthewoso?' she cried joyfully. This was her jokey name for him. She was as tall as him, blonde with an artfully-styled tousled look. He had never figured out her attitude to him, simply been grateful that there was no evident strain between them. She was always friendly and he believed she accepted him. He had never once asked how she saw him, as a stand-in father and a man.

The situation now was a little unnatural, with Cressida watching curiously from a corner. He sensed a certain awkwardness in the air, and was relieved when the house-mate took herself off upstairs.

'That was thoughtful of her,' he said.

'Oh, she is. She always is.'

'There's no need, though. We've got nothing to say that she'd be embarrassed to hear, have we?'

'Of course not,' Marianne said simply, 'but she's like that. As you say, thoughtful.'

'I suppose in a little house like this you have to consider each other more.'

'Yes, that's true. When Sam comes to visit I usually arrange to go to see a friend or a film or something.'

As well as not knowing what her deeper feelings about him were – assuming she was conscious of any – he had always avoided asking her if she felt he was to blame for her mother's death. He wanted desperately to know. Sometimes he had a longing to be blamed, to suffer retribution. And because there was none, that was retribution in itself.

'I hear you've gone to live in the woods, to be a noble savage,' she said, smiling but nice. She wasn't the kind to be sardonic, to take the rise out of anyone. He loved her energy and enthusiasm for life, and wished vainly for a resurgence of his own. She made him dream of his own eager reaching for whatever life offered, so far away now that it was indeed a dream.

'Not noble,' he said. 'I'm not asking for the moon.'

'If it's what you want,' she said, so matter-of-factly that he had an impulse to kiss her.

'Who let you know?'

'Paul, it must have been.'

'I meant to tell you,' he confessed, 'but I thought I'd come instead, and maybe talk about it.'

'You don't have to.'

'No, but I'd like to try.'

She eyed him levelly. 'Have you eaten at all?'

He came out with his prepared idea. 'I thought we could go out for a meal tonight, if you know anywhere small and pleasant.'

'Italian, that do? It's not far – just opened. Five tables, how's that for small? You can take your own wine in.'

'Sounds fine to me.'

'As it happens,' she grinned, 'I've got a bottle, and it's Italian too.'
'What is it?'
'Orvieto.'
'A good one.'
'Right. Give me a few minutes to freshen up. Help yourself to a book or something.'
'Tell Cressida to come down.'
'If she wants to.'
'Of course.'

He was left alone. He thought with heartache of the solitary man, himself, in a rented cottage he called home, a misfit on a farm that was nothing to do with him. He sat tormenting himself with the suspicion that what he had so painfully constructed there out of midnights and dead days was an illusion.

Chapter Eleven

The little restaurant on the Exmouth Road, just opened and eager to please, was empty when they went in. The red and white check tablecloths and the smiling young Italian waiter-owner with the London accent made him feel light-hearted. The Orvieto was handed over and came back at once, uncorked. They both ordered, she a gnocchi and he the cannelloni. The mixed salad was for them to share.

'To the simple life,' he toasted, lifting his glass.

'Yours anyway,' she laughed. 'What do you do with yourself, all alone there?' And sounded truly interested, her straight gaze trying to look into him.

He told her as best he could. 'Not that I'm really alone,' he said. 'You find that out soon enough in the country, when you get away from the noise of streets and traffic. It's all teeming with life round me, even if I don't see most of it.'

'And that's nice?'

'It makes me feel how ignorant I am. What a price we pay for this so-called civilisation.'

'But you've still got your electricity, water and so on, haven't you?'

'Yes, of course,' he admitted. 'There's no going back now, for any of us.'

'So what's the point?' she pressed. Again he felt she was sincerely asking.

'I'm not sure. At first I hated it. Even the silence was horrible, and the dark. Country darkness when it comes down is incredible, it falls over you like a garment. I felt a nobody, nothing, at the edge of the world, about to drop off. Ridiculous when you think that a few miles down the road is a market town.'

She said, as if far away, 'I wonder how I'd cope with it?'

'Then one morning I got up, not wanting to as usual, expecting to feel ghastly, the same dreary emptiness out of the windows, and sitting there over a cup of tea, ready to do the same things desperately again to kill time, to get through, it slowly seeped into me that the horrible silence was in fact a huge unsullied thing, a great invitation, stretching on and on beyond the silence of stars, beyond everything. I don't know how else to put it. I got up and stepped outside, and I was part of it. Mad as this sounds.'

Speaking like this made him apprehensive, and it made him ache to be back there again, entering his journal. To his astonishment he felt the stirring of something else, a poem, a book – what was it? The sensation or whatever it was came complete with label: a missing life. Which was what he was trying, and no doubt failing to communicate. He looked wryly at the girl.

Marianne seemed pleased at any rate to be confided in. Smiling encouragingly she said, 'More wine?'

As the honey-coloured fluid ran into his glass she ordered him to remember the salad. 'Dig in, it's for both of us. Don't you like it?'

'Very much.' Spearing cucumber he asked for something about herself. 'I keep on about me.'

'That's because I keep asking. Are you turning into a mystic?'

He smiled at the word. 'Is that how it sounds? Something equally useless, if not that.'

'I wonder why it's so important for us to know what everyone else does and what it adds up to?' she mused, and then amended with, 'Unless you're caring for someone, trying to rescue them, that sort of thing.'

'How do you view your work?'

'Local radio? Oh, it has its community aspect. You can say it helps lonely people. I don't kid myself though.'

'In what way?'

'I could be subtle but I'm not a subtle type. A lot of it is just noise. I'm in it for the career, for me.'

'Don't put yourself down.'

'I don't,' she said proudly, almost fierce. 'I like what I do. I'm good at it.'

He watched with pleasure as she ate with frank enjoyment, licking her lips and sighing appreciatively.

'Food's important to you,' he said.

She looked startled. 'Oh yes! Why, does it show?'

'In the nicest possible way.'

'Isn't it for you?'

'I didn't think so. Now I'm beginning to get the hang of it.' He laughed at his own absurdity.

She chortled at that. 'I don't remember any difficulty myself. In fact I'm a greedy pig.'

They had come to dessert. She said no with a heavy sigh and settled for coffee. He had an ice-cream and no coffee. 'You're sure you won't have anything else,' he asked.

'I'm trying not to.'

'It's not my talk I hope.'

'Don't over-estimate your influence,' she said teasing gently. He felt a little foolish.

He was aware of her young loveliness. Sometimes it seemed that she was saying one thing and reflecting on another. Did that mean he bored her? He wondered if they would ever speak of Lena's death? Certainly not now. The moment had passed – if there had been such a moment. Was it cowardice on his part that made him think so? He doubted it; his feeling to do so was so intense. What prevented him from broaching the subject was the deep water he would have plunged her in. All at once he veered away inside himself, to the unbroken, age-old silence of the farm's fields and woods.

She asked again how he passed the time.

'Was I evasive when you asked me before?'

'Sketchy,' she said frankly.

He had told her about his writing, the journal as a sort of bridge to his afterlife, attempts at poems and so on, but had played things down. Now he was more honest.

'You must go on with it,' she said suddenly, with urgency. 'The journal thing especially.'

'Why d'you say that?' he asked, because her flare of concern had thrilled him.

'I don't know.' She thought hard, furrowing her brow. 'I suppose it moves me to think of you there, doing that. Trying to make sense of it.'

He asked quietly, 'Why?'

She was at a loss to say more, shrugged and looked helpless, with a funny lopsided grin. 'It just does.'

'Is this the great communicator I'm talking to?'

To his consternation the joke misfired: she looked worried. 'I know. Terrible, isn't it?'

Changing the subject he enquired about her current boyfriend.

She said easily, 'There isn't one, not any more. Francis and I called it a day. Nobody's fault – it just wasn't working. We had different expectations of each other. Other people noticed before we did that there was no future in it for us.' She added ruefully, 'I didn't like his name much – a bad sign.'

'Why?'

'I just didn't.'

'He wasn't a St Francis then.'

'Definitely not.'

'What's wrong with Frank?'

'He wasn't a Frank.'

He was reminded of Cressida, but thought better about saying so. And of Lena, who married at eighteen a kind man she didn't love, had Marianne and then left after a year, unable to face the lie.

'Could it be that you're too fussy?' he asked, nearly adding, 'like your mother'.

'Probably. Both of us have other things we want to do, perhaps that's it. You have to be prepared to make room for someone, and when it came to it we couldn't. I don't know.'

'But you don't feel bad? Now it's over, I mean.'

She said firmly, very brisk. 'No. The opposite. Glad really. Think of all the years we could have wasted. Now the future's open again for me.'

'Sounds wise.'

'I'm a big girl now.'

'How's he taking it?'

'Oh, he feels the same, definitely. Otherwise I'd feel awful. That's how I know.'

'Know what?'

'What d'you think? That he feels as I do.'

He nodded. It was good, so good, how she had turned out. So sure of herself! He said, 'Excuse me if I'm a little slow on the uptake. Let me ask you something else.'

'Go on.'

'Is living a complicated business for you?'

'I wouldn't have thought so once, but now, yes, I *would* say. I suppose the older you get, the more complex it seems.'

'Not only seems.'

She told him he was a good listener, something he had been told before. Partly his focused listening was the result of his inability to engage in small talk. He had noticed how women talked more freely and emotionally with other women, and were surprised to be listened to by men. Most men tended to be dismissive, that seemed a frequent complaint, and if they did talk a lot it was about their boring obsessions.

'Would you like children one day?'

Her laugh was a trifle sour, he thought. She looked sharply at him, gave a small smile and said, as if reluctant to own up to the fact, 'Yes, but it's getting a little late for me now.'

He said, trying to be up-to-date, 'Would you want one if there was no father around?'

'Yes again. That's a strange question.'

'Doesn't it happen now and then these days? I mean the woman giving herself the choice, not seeing the father as part of the deal necessarily.'

The small smile again. 'I wouldn't reject it out of hand, if that's what you're asking.'

'I don't know what I'm asking,' he confessed.

'But you've got me weighed up.'

'Have I?'

Something about his expression made her burst out laughing. He found laughter disconcerting when he didn't know the joke – his insecurity probably – but knew better than to ask: he was thinking of Lena.

Back in her neat little house she gave up her bed for him, sleeping on the couch in the sitting room. He slept fitfully, unable to adjust to the yellow sodium lights from across the road shining against the thin curtains. Cities. He missed the impenetrable wall of silence lowered around his cottage by the night, that he had first feared and hated and now loved. He lay on his back in the morning listening as Cressida went off to her school, hearing the front door, her car door, the engine as she gunned it confidently. Marianne was in the kitchen when he got up.

There was warmth from the radiator in there. He sat by the window and she gave him the cereals he asked for and made tea and toast. She wasn't due in work till noon, but he had decided to start back. He was missing his journal, and the poem idea, if it came to anything, was fermenting in him. It was strange, he told her – when he attempted verse he liked to use the Olivetti, it seemed to encourage the flow. Also it was something to blame. 'When my self-esteem's low I can say it's the machine, not me.'

'How's the self-esteem now?'

'Better, if I can hang on to it.'

'I sometimes think I ought to have something obsessive going on in me, then I remember Francis and his bloody antiques. Everywhere we went he'd be hunting them down. What is it about men?'

'You don't envy us then?' he joked.

'God no.'

'Somebody said, some sage or other, that a woman's aim in life is always completion, wholeness, while the man is forever trying to get born properly.'

She crunched at her toast, comically serious. 'I'll think about it.'

'I envy women their ability to act spontaneously.'

'Don't idealise us. Always a big mistake.'

'I'll remember,' he said with a smile. 'From the horse's mouth.'

'This horse anyway.'

Her warning struck home in him. Wordsworth, he recalled, spoke of his need to grip a gate in order to avoid falling in to what he called the 'abyss of idealism'.

Saying goodbye, he was treated again to her indiscriminate generous embrace. He refused to let her take him to the station, saying he preferred to walk. The truth was he could barely speak, stricken by a turmoil of emotion brought on by the farewell, by his step-daughter's warmth and fragrance, by the feeling he had of being brushed by Lena, touched on the cheek and then abandoned. He walked along with his head down, tears pressing up behind his eyes.

Chapter Twelve

He broke his journey at Cheltenham and visited the grave, even though on his trip to see Paul and Hilary he had been there. The avenue of trees had lost its leaves. Only one person was about, a man, near Lena's headstone. Coming close, Hopkin saw that he was planting hardy pansies, on his knees wielding a trowel. Big shoulders, ham hands. They met at the tap, the Irishman saying how many people young lay dead in this part of the cemetery. Hopkin said that yes, he'd noticed. The big fellow really wanted to speak of his son, dead at thirty after hanging himself. He came out with it in a rush, like something pouring out of him he couldn't control. The man's wife had died some months before. Now here he was putting flowers on a grave for his family. Hopkin was shocked.

As the man waited almost hungrily for a word of comment, Hopkin ventured to ask whether the son had left a note.

'He'd just come back from a holiday in Scotland, youth hostelling with a friend. He said in his note that he was sorry, Dad, he couldn't cope any more. With what? Every day I ask that question.'

'Terrible, all wrong,' Hopkin found himself mumbling.

The stranger shook his head. 'It is, it is. I shouldn't be coming here, should I, to somebody that young. I shouldn't be the one that's left, now should I? I come here three times a week,' he went on, 'in my lunch hour mostly. My boss, he don't mind if I stay a bit late, I make it up for him, he knows that. He can trust me. He's all right.'

In Hopkin's hand as he listened was the chrome flower container. When the other man left him he cleaned and freshened it with the icy tap water, then returned to the grave-side. He had thought to bring a newspaper with him to kneel on as the ground was muddy. Like the Irishman nearby to his left he knelt down, breaking off the stalks of his bronze chrysanthemums with his hand before arranging them. He wanted them to fan out evenly, feeling absurdly agitated when they didn't.

At last it was done. The stone said, 'To a beloved wife, loved in death as in life.' He feared that it might not be true in time to come, as she slipped with her loved shape and the sound of her voice gradually beyond his reach. This was a bitter thought and he always blamed himself. Another bitterness was the stone mason's mistake: the inscription should have read 'my beloved'. This had seemed nothing at the time, but had since grown huge. He turned away, the darkly blazing flower heads, when he glanced back at them, challenging him to keep her living always, in every aspect. Rain began falling sharply as he hurried out.

Back at last, tramping up the long drive of loose shale and potholes between dripping poplars, the firs of the wood standing mysteriously dim to his right, he realised he was starting to think of the place as his, even though it would never belong to him. He had tentatively sounded out the farmer on the question of selling the cottage some time in the future but Symonds, saying what he meant as usual, was adamant: the only person he would consider was someone dedicated to the cause who would be a helper. And helping meant hard slog, every day and at weekends. Hopkin didn't need telling. It wasn't him, and he was too old. In any case Symonds preferred to rent, keeping control and avoiding problems such as dogs, children – especially dogs worrying his sheep.

The mud-splattered Landrover jolting along on the drive towards him must be Michael, he guessed; and he was right. It pulled up beside him and the cultivated voice asked after his health.

'Glad to be back. I'm fine.'

'Good, good. We've kept an eye on things for you. You'll find dry wood by the boiler and plenty of logs stacked in the barn for you to go at.'

He had abandoned the cursed boiler for good, but kept quiet about it. He didn't want another lesson in boiler-firing. 'That's nice of you,' he said warmly, and meant it. 'Where are you off to now?'

'More logging. Want to come along?'

Hopkin shook his head. 'Not dressed for it. Thanks again.'

Ducking his head shyly, Michael asked about Hopkin's grandson.

'All's well now. It wasn't meningitis as they'd dreaded. The symptoms were misleading.'

The man at the wheel damped down his interest with unerring good taste, nodded stiffly and let in the clutch. Hopkin went on with a spring in his step, forgetting the ache in his thighs and calves. His breath was visible in the frosty air.

Next morning he was up at eight, still tired but quietly rejoicing in his surroundings, suppressing an urge to go thumping along through the wood, alone and thankful to be. He sat gazing out of the glass wall of the conservatory with his elbows on the table – he had dragged the drop-leaf table from the cramped kitchen where there was no view out and placed it on the bare concrete of the conservatory, if he could dignify the spider-infested boiler-room with such a name. For heating he had a two-bar electric fire with a rusty reflector, close by his legs. He had tried sitting at the front window and felt the thread connecting him with the occasional customer driving past to buy meat. It was distracting, even when nothing happened, so he turned his back on it, happy instead to face the animistic wood. Primitive man believed that natural objects were the dwelling places of spirits. If Lena was living on somewhere, why not out there, in the heart of the wood?

He drank tea, switched on the radio for the pleasure of switching off, the better to savour the intense stillness, then slipped outside and stood at the wire fence admiring one lolloping young pig, which advanced towards him, ambling and curious like a cow, then veered away to start rooting in the ground. The wind was non-existent; not a leaf, not a blade stirring. He made himself stand where he was and let the spell of it all take hold of him. He wished he could disconnect his mind for an hour, a day. Then he felt the pallid tendril of a poem unwinding out of some dark recess in his chest and ran back inside to get out the typewriter.

He sat again at the deal table that was cleared of breakfast, paper wound into the machine, his acute nervousness telling him that this might be it. He was ready to accept any offering, black or burning bright. Whatever reached the light would go down, and he would take a vow not to tamper with it, other than what was necessary to deliver it cleanly and purely.

Forgetting at last his tattered self he felt an influx of power, the power of the moment. He caught himself swaying his body back and forth on his hard chair like a tense driver, and finally postponed the poem long enough to write down in clear words the argument for the whole hoped-for work, stamping out heavily in bold capitals A MISSING LIFE and then trying to pin down just what that meant.

When he conceived it on his travels to Cheltenham and Exeter he'd believed he meant Lena, the great gaping wound, and yes he did. Even as he affirmed the fact he was being led to an awareness of his own lost life, in the grave with his dead wife but also in the grave of his hopes, his youth, his dreams: in short, the life he had mislaid and soiled and made ragged in streets, while the real life was elsewhere and waiting like those trees shrouded in mist, standing through time with their endless patience. He had read somewhere that trees were once sacred, worshipped by our ancestors, who built temples and then cathedrals echoing in their forms the sacred groves. Once, forests covered the land solidly from northern Europe to the Mediterranean, and the word savage had its origin in 'from the trees'.

All his days he had been a tree-worshipper without knowing it. For the ancient Greeks, gods lived among trees. He could believe it. Aborigines and Red Indians went in awe of trees, building fires in them to release their spirits. Hopkin sat in his quietude telling himself that this was literary nonsense à la Rousseau, and then was gladdened by the steadfast gloom and unshakeable reality of the wood before him. It was there, it would be there long after he was gone, it had a presence that was sombre, hoary, out of reach of our comprehension; old and yet virginal. 'I want to paint the earth's virginity,' said bad-tempered Cézanne, a man of few words. Hopkin thought of desecrations, his own on himself, the world on trees.

Typing, he began to wonder whether his poem called for a prose commentary of some kind running along in parallel. He let that hang in the air unresolved, called a halt to speculation and swiftly composed a thing of fear and longing that was almost automatic writing so far as he was concerned.

> Early mornings can bring a dread
> but there is nothing to tell.
> Without name or face, it sends me
> burrowing in vain.
>
> Something lies in wait. And yet
> your smile does good –
> if you would only wake.
>
> This is where love starts,
> the futile swarming of cities
> stilled by a breath.
>
> Far off, our bodies lie together
> as they once did.
> Gardens fill with birds
> in the noise and waste of this age.

A pricking behind the eyes brought on by 'if you would only wake' convinced him that something at least was truly felt. Apart from that he was at first sadly disappointed by the brevity and slightness of his verse. He saw he had spoken as though his wife was still alive, and while the act of writing possessed him she was. It was no surprise that he had addressed it to her: she had always been his first, sometimes his only reader.

He remembered his vow not to lose faith in what came, read his lines again and began to feel encouraged. During the morning he must have come back to his folder a dozen times. He took the no longer pristine paper out and examined it yet again before a bite of lunch, knowing he would be compelled to come back many more times yet. This reassured him, sufficiently at any rate to know he would have to go on. If he was this obsessed, it meant he was serious. A Missing Life was going to be reclaimed, reunited with its author, who in the first flush of his creation felt he was being given another chance. What else was art for, if not to rehabilitate you, and through you, others?

He was wary of being pretentious, as well as presumptuous, on the basis of a handful of words. His thoughts went on circling and returning to his frail paper boat on which the cindery marks had fallen, indelible as a tattoo. He did a little prose musing on another sheet of paper, that he thought might link any other poems that came in a series. Would they arrive? To give himself a break from it all he shrugged on his duffle coat and marched out for a walk.

The twilight was already gathering, and seemed like something the host of trees churned out soundlessly in their creaking solitude. He blinked, shook his head, rubbed his forehead in a daze. Where had the day gone? He loved the pure, purple gravity of the dusk. The air was cold and hung immobile, brushing against his face with a current so gentle that the drops of water everywhere stayed put. After the heyday of his words he felt an urge to plunge into those groves, but was afraid he might meet disillusionment. Also, if he was honest, the thought of the thickening darkness if he blundered among those trees scared him. Instead he left the drive starred with cow shit and climbed straight up over the rough backside of the open field, on the crest of which were a dozen wary sheep getting ready to scatter as he went stumbling higher.

As he climbed and his breath rasped painfully in his chest, reminding him of his age, he marvelled at his new-found eagerness to write and the renewal of his belief in it. It had always been there, but undermined by Academe, and not only that. Where was the validity of art any more? Conscious of so much injustice, cruelty, torture, so many empty bellies, what was his excuse?

In the past his itch to write had filled him with obscure resentment. He had thought freedom was the answer. His one wretched affair had not really been about the girl but what he imagined she represented, freedom, a chance to live without ties like a gypsy, a chance to be himself. She wore hippie beads but was no gypsy, and in fact longed for what he had with his wife. He soon discovered she was less free than himself, less together than his wife, and as a final bitter joke had looked to him to grant her the freedom she thought she wanted. Those few bitter days away and occasional visits had made him feel so bad about himself that the desire to write was killed stone dead. He shuddered even now to think of how repulsive the blank page had looked to him. He would break into a sweat, he wept in front of it. Soon he was breaking down.

When he came to the top of the ridge and stood admiring the beauty below, which the dying light did nothing to diminish, the wood somehow bulkier than ever with its freight of dusk, he told himself that just as one didn't question the value of being alone, or ask what its purpose was in this hurrying world, one didn't either put a price on the peace that passes understanding, that peace of mind he had once disastrously lost after lying to his wife.

It was only when he began to write again at weekends that he understood again what had driven him, always: his baby son quivering in the bath as he was gently lowered and sluiced, wonderment piercing the new father with delight; his wife closing her eyes during love to give herself totally, as he lay above her dying and getting reborn; the unspoken grace and thankfulness of the evening meals. He wasn't saying that his writing was about that, but it was what nourished it, drove it. What it was about he would rather not try to know. Some words by the painter Dubuffet a friend had quoted to him once in a letter remained with him, how accurately he couldn't be sure: 'Art doesn't lie down in the bed that is made for it: it runs away as soon as one says its name: it loves to be incognito.'

He was glad to leave it at that. To be incognito was his aim too, with art and his life married indissolubly, running hand in hand. This was so fanciful that he nearly laughed aloud. And with a mere slip of a poem to show.

The folded valley below him was now funeral-grey, as the light faded. He was above the trees of the wood, looking over their tops, and he stood peacefully above the little world he now knew, the roof of his cottage, the barns, the drive, lying deserted below. He stood waiting and listening, at peace with himself and spellbound.

Preoccupied now with his desire to write he would pick a book up in the library, say a novel, and open it at random. Tags he mopped up like this, magpie fashion, he carried back to his retreat, leaving the book on the shelf. In one, by a Jewish writer who was either a charlatan or a magician, he could never decide, he read a scrap of doggerel and the words 'Hide in your hole', and something about dread, which rhymed with 'gnaw your bread'. So he went back to his hole, to gnaw his bread and fight his dread.

The second poem came a few days later of its own volition, his imagination suddenly pouring. When that happened he didn't care about the paucity of the result, or whether it was despairing or joyous. The flow itself was joyous enough, no matter what was said. Later came the questions, the doubt.

The last thing he wanted was to sit there each morning demanding action, he told himself. Results of themselves were not the point. You could do that with prose but not poetry. All the same he was growing uneasy, doing his best not to panic. A voice warned him that it would be so easy to fall back into the deathly state of his first weeks here, not to mention before he came. Nor did he want to see his theme of a missing life, which when he hit on it seemed to embrace everything, his lost wife, lost way, lost earth, to be a kind of formula for resurrecting Lena and saying to her all the things he had meant and failed to say. To do so would be forcing, faking. The art Dubuffet evoked would be scared off and go chasing down the drive or into the trees, never to be seen again. He had this comical image of a figure running with its trousers falling down.

Like a train arriving from an unknown destination – he had used the image before to convey the mystery of it – with snow on the carriage roofs, into a station where there had been no snowfall, the poem slid in. Again he transcribed it as though taking dictation, dismayed at first by the implicit gloom but still firm in his resolve to accept and keep faith with what he was given, complete with title in this case. He tinkered hardly at all.

> DUMBSTRUCK
> Nothing for it
> when you are full of unlived life
> but to go on
> dreaming of nakedness,
> abandonment, the flesh that overpowers,
> fills the hands, stops the mouth.
> Nothing for it
> in the cold ash of dawn
> but to get out of bed
> and stop remembering
> the wild woods
> of the heart's springtime.

> Dumbstruck to find
> nothing had changed.
> We go on, then, to the end,
> weighed down by centuries,
> believing everything and nothing.
> Weary unto death
> we reach out. We hope.

This time he didn't keep trailing back to his folder like a dog to its vomit but left it hidden like a bone and hurried out into the fresh air; very fresh. As the bitter cold he hadn't realised was there slapped him he gasped. It was a strong wind with teeth from the northeast, diving under his coat and causing him to shove his hands deep in his pockets. All the same, after being so deeply inside himself he was eager to jump out. He imagined coming up from a coalmine: the huge light and space surprised him. He would have liked human company, but there was none.

In the distance he could hear the handsome creamy white bull roaring, the one they called Pedro, down near the road. He guarded three cows, all with names, in a field Hopkin had once thought to cross. He put a foot on the fence and threw one leg over. Pedro, who was reputed to be soft as butter, lowered his broad shaggy head and began moving with alarming speed in his direction. Hopkin, a townie after all, changed his mind. Another time he found the great animal standing docilely where he wasn't supposed to be, on the coarse grass in front of his cottage. It was late evening. The beast loomed out in the darkness, a monument in white. His admirer from a safe distance gazed in astonishment from the window, on the point of drawing the curtains. Outside, he skirted him gingerly and went off to the farmhouse to report his find.

PART THREE

SPIRIT OF THE WOODS

Chapter Thirteen

One Tuesday he was coming in around noon from a shopping trip, rucksack bouncing on his back. Making his way round the side to the door into the yawning empty kingdom of the boiler, which always managed to accuse him silently of neglect, he thought that Michael had probably guessed he had given up on it and was too well-bred to say. Passing it, Hopkin let his gaze slide obsessively over that great rounded iron bulk. It was crazy but he had to stop himself from touching it like an animal he felt bound to placate. Even dormant it exuded power, reminding him of a locomotive stalled on its tracks.

He unpacked his groceries in the kitchen, cursing himself for forgetting eggs. These days his memory was full of holes, clouded too no doubt by his concentrating on writing. What sort of farm was this, without hens and fresh-laid eggs? There it was: though he did get his milk, knocking at the side door of the house for it. The door led into a scullery pungent with the smell of milk. That was another mystery – it was always deaf Mrs Symonds who answered, shaking her head if he offered money, smiling him away with some words about the weather. How had she heard? He always forgot to hammer harder, then remembered and before he could raise his fist again the door was opening.

About to settle down to some writing in the conservatory he stopped, cocked an ear, sure he could hear a noise, the sound of someone or something humming. It stopped. He went outside and reconnoitred, peering around corners, expecting to see Michael. When he got back to his workplace and wound paper into the machine, the humming started again. Definitely human.

He rubbed at his ears and concentrated. Nothing. Then more humming. He ventured outside to explore again, skirted the brick and glass wall until he came to a small compound choked full of rubbish, a decaying fowlpen, wire netting, a sheet of rusted-out corrugated iron, all tangled with weeds and brambles. Beyond that was an outhouse lean-to, built against the end wall of the cottage. He had once peered into it, scraping off cobwebs from the glass with the back of his hand to see an interior jammed with lumber, an old kitchen sink, an ancient electric cooker. The Symonds family ran a spick-and-span establishment, the cleanest farmyard he had seen, but this heap of junk was out of sight and no doubt forgotten. The humming started up again.

Hopkin was at the dirty cobwebbed glass like a Peeping Tom and what he saw gave him a nasty shock. A young man was crouched over a makeshift table with his back to him, humming loudly. For a seat he had piled up some split logs – *his* logs! The lumber had been shoved over to one side to give him space: even so he was wedged in with no room to move. His table was an old splintery door, propped at one end by the chipped yellow sink turned on its side and at the other by more logs, piled against the outside cottage wall. Hopkin was about to cough or bang on something, but something about the man's bent concentrated shoulders stopped him, and reminded him of himself – hunched like a warning sign: do not disturb. What was he doing, bent over a pad of lined A4, grimy and scrawled over in thick black pencil or crayon? As Hopkin spied and felt furtive the pencil paused, scratched out with an angry gesture and went racing on, the writing so large he could almost make out words from where he stood.

Before the oblivious intruder came up for air and turned, Hopkin had taken in the Rasta plaits dangling from a black greasy head. He half expected a Caribbean face – though that would have been unlikely round here – but it was white, bony and abstracted, the eyes staring without alarm, so that Hopkin, furious at having his seclusion invaded and then anxious because it might be put at risk if it was thought he had invited someone without permission, was wrong-footed.

Instead of asking indignantly who the hell he was and what was going on, he found himself asking foolishly, his voice mild, curious even, 'What are you doing?' His voice sounded small and unwilling in his own ears.

'Can I talk to you in a bit,' the fellow said, in his twenties Hopkin guessed, and went on guessing, he thought futilely; but in one respect his guess was accurate. He had smelled woodsmoke on the other's clothes, caught no doubt in the ragged wool of his sweater, rainbow-coloured, that looked as if it had been gnawed into holes at the elbows. Not waiting for a reply the man turned back to his task and went on covering paper. 'Jimmy's my name,' he mumbled over his shoulder, a complaint in his voice that he should have to bother. 'Jimmy Plant.'

Hopkin went back inside with his jumbled emotions and a new problem. He made himself a coffee, boiling the water and then filling the mug a third full of milk and taking it back to the stove, where he boiled it on the hotplate, a procedure his wife had found mystifying. It comforted him somehow, except when the saucepan boiled over. He thought of making coffee for the stranger, telling himself not to be an idiot, that it would be stupid and compromising. His mind working non-stop, he wondered if the fellow had got permission from Mr Symonds or perhaps Michael to use the outhouse, and got angry again to think that if so, he hadn't been consulted. But the whole idea was ridiculous. Like his temper the milk and water rose in the saucepan and he caught it in the nick of time. Wasn't the whole point of his being here the solitude and the flight from people? He'd explain how it was to this person trespassing and tell him politely to shove off, find some other hole to crawl into. And why here? Working himself up again he reflected that all his life he had failed to assert himself and consequently been walked over, bending to the whims of others, anything for a quiet life, earning himself the reputation at work of a nice inoffensive character who would be the last one to object to anything. Only at home had he shown his true colours, once or twice shamefully.

The scribbling maniac who squatted outside was, he felt sure, one of the New Agers who had established a colony of clapped-out trucks, buses and caravans along a strip of land they had managed to infiltrate last summer down by the river. He had heard the talk in pubs. The council were supposed to be taking action but were hoping the winter weather or flood water would save them the trouble. Often apparently they arrived in this area and then six months later had gone. This time it hadn't happened. Speculating on the attitude of the Symondses he imagined the doughty old farmer would approve of the anti-establishment stance of New Age travellers, but in theory, from a distance. For one thing there was the menace of their dogs; they always had mongrels wandering loose. No, he'd give short shrift to anyone squatting on his property, Hopkin decided.

His days, which had seemed up to now blissfully free of problems, now had one looming over them. He was cast into shadow. He had to get rid of this mystery writer. An inner voice was saying, 'First of all find out what he's writing. Fellow addicts at least deserve a hearing.' Not that this one seemed in any hurry to look for a reader, or to introduce himself even. Hopkin emerged and approached the outhouse warily, half expecting or hoping the place to be vacated. No, the man who called himself Jimmy was, large as life, still bent to his task. Hopkin banged accidentally on purpose against a rotting fence rail.

The ghost writer stopped. Threw down his pencil as if disgusted. Twisted round on his tottery stool. He jabbed a finger at his pad of paper and said grimly, 'This bastard mess is going to be a book, mate. You see if it ain't.' He seemed to be threatening his own work rather than addressing his visitor. 'I'm Matthew Hopkin,' Hopkin said, feeling elderly, about to move forward and stick out his hand but thinking better of it.

'I know who you are.'

This took the older man's breath away. He stammered, 'You do? Who told you?'

'You're a writer, right?'

Hopkin was embarrassed. He had never solved the question of identity. His instinct was always to deny an interest. 'Not professionally,' he began to say.

'Who gives a shit about that?' Jimmy said, his voice surly. 'I've heard your typer goin'.'

Still nonplussed, Hopkin said that yes, as a matter of fact he had launched out on something that might amount to something, but he was nervous of talking about it specifically just yet.

'That's my feeling about this thing,' Jimmy confided. 'All I can say at the moment is it's goin' to be big.'

Hopkin's heart sank. Swerving round this subject that he felt was compromising him more deeply with every word, he asked Jimmy where he lived, and wasn't surprised to hear him say down by the river. 'Only I can't get private enough there. I was scoutin' around like and then heard you pounding out your screed.'

Hopkin was unsure of his ground and how to continue. 'Where did you find out my name?' he asked. 'From the Symondses?'

'Don't know any Symondses.'

'They own this farm, this cottage, this place you're sitting in.'

Jimmy contrived to look down his nose and amused at the same time. 'This rathole?'

'All the same.'

It was extraordinary, Hopkin should have been the irritated one and here was this character looking distinctly impatient. He said now, with an edge to his voice, 'No sweat. Say the word and I'll piss off out of here.'

'I'm not saying that.' Though he was thinking and hoping.

The fellow twisted back round, his voice floating up. 'I'm wrestlin' with something hard, you know? Talk to you later, okay, if you've nothing better to do.'

'Right.'

Hopkin retreated, feeling dismissed, suppressing anger at that 'if you've nothing better to do' line. Back at his table by the conservatory glass he found himself unable to function, his mind veering about, skittering like an alarmed bird and always coming down to perch in a tree near the outhouse, a dump he had hardly noticed and now was beginning to curse. He concentrated, sweated with useless effort before his own project and then stood up groaning, taut in his nerves, and went out for a walk, tramping along blind down the drive and then off to the left into the trees. In a sudden rage he crashed through the undergrowth, choosing the most impenetrable gaps, slithering to a stop down a bank in a clearing where a spring trickled. He must have been here before but he felt strange, a stranger. The wood was excluding him. He sat on a mossy stump and considered the morning's events. The sane thing was to do nothing, to wait and see. If you can't decide, can't reach a decision, do nothing. It was sound advice. He felt a renewed spurt of rage because he was no longer incognito, that blessed state. 'I know who you are' sounded ominous, upsetting him more than anything else. Just how did this Jimmy Plant know? And why in God's name did it matter anyway?

Retracing his steps, blundering around at one point because he was temporarily lost, he reasoned calmly that tomorrow he could well wake up and find himself alone and everything as it had been. Jimmy was young and the young were notoriously restless, hopping like fleas from one mania to another. Soon it would be freezing cold, and nobody could work without heat in that draughty shed. Just to think of it put a chill on your mind. Also he would need food and drink, and a toilet.

He began to feel triumphant. By the time he got back he was almost good-tempered. About to enter his side door into the glass cavern, the boiler's home rather than his, he stood listening intently. No humming. Holding his breath he crept nearer, trying not to snap twigs under his gumboots. He was aware of how ridiculous he must look, sneakily reconnoitring round his own legitimate place of residence. He reached the outhouse, peeked in through the dirty pane of glass. Empty. His heart leapt. He was free again.

He entered the fusty, cobwebby space with a curious sensation of guilt. The A4 pad had gone and the pencil, but the rickety table-door was still in position. He stood with his head cocked, thinking. Back inside his own refuge, which had now taken on a cosy, luxurious look, so that he felt absurdly privileged and glad, he sawed at his granary loaf and made a thick sandwich of sliced beetroot, with a stick of celery and a piece of Cheddar on the side. He poured his usual gassy mineral water into a tumbler, and again felt pampered, vaguely uneasy.

In the afternoon he approached his work table in a sideways crab-like movement, as if not to do anything serious, sat down and made his second attempt of the day. It came out constipated, so he gave up for the present and tried to read. From Stroud library, which he had recently joined, he had got out a life of Chekhov. He had never been a theatregoer, somehow put off and embarrassed by actors, by their shameless egotism – as was Chekhov himself he was learning – but he liked to read plays. Was it O'Neill who never went to see his own plays performed? The great Russian's stories were largely unknown to him and he planned to remedy that, for he was finding out that the man was endearing, so modest, never believing in his own importance, always burdening himself with the cares of others and yet curiously remote, cold even. He spoke longingly of solitude and yet lived in the midst of friends and relatives. All the warmth in him ran into his work, though he spoke of composing as an act calling for icy reserve, detaching himself almost inhumanely to write scenes of pathos and passion. Hopkin, losing himself in the enigma of Chekhov, forgot his own troubles. When he remembered them he saw them as ludicrous.

The next morning he woke with a sensation of not being alone, resisted the urge to investigate till he had had his breakfast and then marched round with some purpose. He hoped to find nothing but if the stranger was there he'd have it out with him, no dithering, explaining bluntly why there was no future in the arrangement so far as he was concerned.

Emptiness. He went back in, expecting to be elated, and to his consternation felt a definite pang of disappointment. He shook his head in disgust, calling himself every kind of fool. Didn't he realise how lucky he was? Though still adamant that it couldn't have continued, all the same he would have liked to know more.

For instance, what kind of book was Jimmy working on – and he had said *book*, a word that reverberated. After all, he knew nothing about him, no clue as to why the writing was so important to such an unlikely looking character, assuming it was. He looked in deadly earnest: no arguing with that.

There could, he reasoned, be interesting parallels with his own motives. Though he hugged his own solitude possessively, it was impossible not to want to discuss these matters with a fellow practitioner if the opportunity had presented itself. It might have done so, given time, though he doubted it. It had only been possible with one person in his long experience, and that was his stricken friend Bill. And how could he discuss anything with him now, a man hanging by his fingernails, who felt unbearably crippled in all areas of his life, lacerating himself with the conviction that when creativity failed he was as good as dead: worse, one of the living dead. Weren't there innumerable ways of being creative, open to all? Jimmy Plant might have been a trifle belligerent on first acquaintance, but Hopkin hadn't detected any real bitterness stemming from self-loathing in the fleeting contact he'd had with him.

He got down to his own work, entering the strange encounter in his journal, and had reached mid morning and was making coffee with kettle and saucepan when the sound of singing reached him. In spite of himself his heart gladdened. He took a grip, sat calmly with his mug of milky coffee, drank it down with a steady hand, then went to see if his fellow writer would fancy a drink.

Jimmy was crouched over as before, hard at it. A tuft of black hair stuck up like a feather on the crown of his head. His observer was touched for some reason. The day was frosty and he wore fingerless mittens, and sat in his mud-stained army surplus greatcoat. Last of the Mohicans. Hopkin, imagination running, thought he looked medieval somehow.

Asked if he'd like something to drink, he said tea without lifting his head.

'Sugar, milk?' his host asked meekly, aware of the part he was playing and curious to see where it would lead him.

'Three sugars,' the committed writer said, without stopping.

Hopkin came back with the mug of tea and placed it beside the scribbling hand, which suddenly stopped, the back straightening. Jimmy showed his face.

'If you need the toilet,' Hopkin began.

'No sweat.'

The invaded man, who had lain in bed the night before composing a letter of reasoned objection which he'd intended leaving on the table-door, afterwards rejecting the idea as cowardly, asked the youngster how long he thought his masterpiece would take, except that the word masterpiece stayed in his head.

'How would I know?'

'What is it, a novel?' He didn't say autobiography, which would have been precocious in the extreme for one so young, though of course first novels were invariably autobiographical. He had once talked in a tutorial to a dreamy student who, like Jimmy, was writing a sort of book, about the difference between autobiography and writing autobiographically. The student half listened, obviously bored, not getting it. The difference the lecturer was labouring was too subtle or beside the point.

'A book,' Jimmy Plant said.

Hopkin was becoming conscious of the possibility that this budding author who had staked a claim on his territory, had perhaps moved in specifically to be near him, the maker of busy typewriter noise if nothing else. Someone who was even vaguely engaged on the same activity, for whatever reason, did give him a boost. On the other hand, to look at him sitting there without a blush or a blink, his thighs arrogantly spread, you wouldn't exactly think in terms of a kindred spirit. But if he was serious, and he surely was – or why suffer this freezing hovel? – then they had something in common. Loneliness?

He said carefully, unable to resist asking, hearing the silly deference in his voice, 'Do you have a title for it?'

'Why?' Jimmy asked, as suspicious as if he'd been stopped by the police.

'Well,' Hopkin fumbled, 'I don't know about you, but in my case it helps. Gives a sort of shape to whatever it is you hope to compose. Anyway, I have to admit I like titles. Like frames round a picture.'

'What picture? Didn't I say I only started it last week?'

'No, you didn't.'

Jimmy held up the pad and flicked the pages. It dropped down on the table like a wounded bird. 'Ten pages is all I've done.'

'You seem to be going at a fair lick,' Hopkin said admiringly.

'I cross out as much as I write. More.'

'I've got sympathy with you over that. It shows you know what you don't want, even if you can't always reach what you do want.'

Jimmy was eyeing the other man with curiosity, if not respect. 'You a teacher or what?'

'Not any more. I retired early.'

'To write your book?'

Hopkin, with the great gulf of years and happenings between them, tried to be as truthful as he could under the circumstances. 'No. That came after. You may think this is weird, but I'm where you are. I only started mine last week. Before that I was writing a private journal.'

'And now it's what?'

He struggled to say, self-consciously using words like poems and prose, until the stranger cut him short. 'What did you specialise in, when you did teachin' for a living?'

'English literature, at a Poly.'

'Teachers got on my tits when I was at school.'

'Same here.'

'Don't you have a woman around?'

'My wife died.' Hopkin, disliking the tone and the impudence, refused to elaborate.

'What of?' his amazed ears heard Jimmy say, as if passing time or speaking of the weather.

'I prefer not to talk about it. Nobody's business but mine.' He found such direct confrontation hard for him and always had, his face hot, his voice strangling.

'Right on,' Jimmy said mildly. There was a funny silence and then he said in the same disengaged voice, 'This bullshit about titles and frames is no use to me.'

'Forget it, then.'

'It's forgot. Why are you so hung up on labels anyway? Prose, poetry. Novel, not-novel. Is that the price you pay for being a teacher?'

"Ex-teacher.'

'Is it?'

'Probably.'

Hopkin looked to see if by the other's face there was humour somewhere, since he could detect none in the voice. Jimmy was deadpan, evidently pursuing his own train of thought and considering the relevance of what was said to his own problems. Anyone who wrote had problems, of that Hopkin was absolutely sure; though what kind of problems and why he would have been hard pressed to explain.

'I'm learning as I go along.'

Surprised by this modest admission, Hopkin agreed wholeheartedly that it was the only attitude to take. 'I did the same. Still do.'

Another pregnant pause. Jimmy turned back to his labour, then swung round again. 'Thanks, dad,' he said, with a grin that said it all.

This aroused the other's ire, but he wasn't one to show it, or say so. Instead he said softly and maliciously, 'You'll need a title when you start looking for a publisher.'

He had struck home, and was instantly ashamed of himself. Jimmy's face darkened. He spat out, 'Who gives a shit about publishers and what they want?' In his rage he swayed unsteadily on his perch. 'I know nobody's interested in what I put down and that's why I'm finding it fucking hard, not writing to please, saying something unique to me. My story. That only I can tell. How I see it, not how some arsehole of a critic would like it to be. Every time I write a sentence that looks approvable I scratch it out. Get it? I'm not stupid, I've turned over books in libraries, I've read the papers. The only way for me to express things is by using sheer rage, and that's what I'm doin'. Get it?'

Hopkin nodded. He was well aware of the need to tread gently; his years of dealing with the tender susceptibilities of students had taught him that. Yet Jimmy was rubbed raw by something, that was clear, more so than any ego-bound student he had come across. Something in Hopkin, perhaps a core of buried rage of his own, never let out or allowed a voice, was responding as he listened to this tirade. He envied the other's passion. Life is short and you have to seize it, as all the poets have testified. Lawrence, for instance, half dead, never stopped demanding more life.

Envying, he stood as if stuck, nailed to the dirty plank floor behind Jimmy Plant who had again presented his back. He wouldn't have changed places with him, his own youth had been too excruciating, but the energy was enviable. Kept there by his curiosity, above all he had to get it off his chest about the difficulty, impossibility of the situation as it affected him. He was tempted to fall into the other's lingo and accuse out loud, 'Not that you give a shit.' Instead he waited obstinately, forcing the busy writer to pay attention by sheer force of will. Jimmy stopped, threw down his pencil. 'I'll be glad to pass the time of day or whatever when I've done my stint,' he griped. 'Look Hopkin, you may be lonely, mate, but I gotta get going.'

Hopkin spoke over lumps half blocking his throat. 'No, now. It's important.' In spite of his difficulty in speaking when upset or enraged he still wondered what his opponent was like physically, how tall and so on. He had only seen him seated, drowning in thick clothes. By his face he guessed he was skinny. Did he have short legs, a modern-day Balzac?

Jimmy, wanting to know what was important, screwed up his face derisively. 'Let me guess,' he said, his drawl insolent.

'You're not the only one who wants to work,' Hopkin got out.

'What's stoppin' you?'

'In short, you.'

Hopkin's heart was pounding. He tried to calm down his breathing. 'This isn't my style,' he confessed. 'I've got plenty of sympathy for what you're trying to do, though why it has to be here baffles me. Where do you live, what's wrong with it there?'

'I told you that. No peace and quiet. The kids I hang out with at the moment never stop banging on about the state of society, materialism, all that. Know any New Agers?'

Hopkin confessed that his knowledge, such as it was, came from journalism.

'They mean well but they never stop yapping. They keep trying to convert me but I'm not interested. It's their grief, I've got my own. I've got better things to do with my time.'

'Lawrence could write in the corner of a room full of people yammering away apparently.'

'Who?'

'D.H. Lawrence.'

'Jesus, I thought you were on about a mate of yours.'

'Look, it's none of my business what your problems with other people are,' Hopkin ground out, beginning to shake, cursing himself for getting overwrought. 'My problem isn't you, no. It's that I came here with the deliberate intention of burying myself away from everybody, for personal reasons I don't care to go into.'

From the other's unfriendly silence he gathered he was not winning. It was now or never, so he kept going. To speak forthrightly he always had to go over the edge, which made him shiver from head to foot. Jimmy observed him shuddering.

'You got a chill?'

'No, I'm fine.'
'Finished your spiel?'
'Not yet.'
'Keep on, then, if it makes you feel any better.'
'How do you get in here? Up the drive in full view?'
'Of the rabbits and cows?'
'It's no joke.'

Jimmy's face took on a sly, ancient expression. If he wasn't New Age, what then? Something much older, gypsy stock? He said confidently, 'I got my own way.'

'You could still be seen, by Symonds' son Michael, by the cowman, by the old man himself. They're all around, working, they could be anywhere.'

'Never seen a soul.'

'Then you're lucky.'

'Stop worrying, mate, nobody's going to see me. Aren't you allowed visitors or something? What are you, in purdah?'

Hopkin sucked in a deep breath in another effort to cool down. 'Of course nobody objects to people calling on me, but this is different. You're hidden away here – '

'Like somebody on the run,' Jimmy finished, coldly contemptuous. 'Tough shit.'

Floundering on with increasing difficulty, Hopkin said wildly, 'Michael calls in here sometimes, I never know when.' It sounded pathetic but he kept on. 'What if he hears you humming and singing away?'

'Stop beating about the fucking bush. If you don't want me here, say so. You won't see me again, I'll melt into nowhere. My enchanting company will be yours no more, it's your loss. Make up your mind.'

'If this was my place there'd be no problem,' Hopkin said, the lie unpleasant on his tongue. 'I'm being straight with you. It's a matter of protecting my position.' And my own peace of mind he could have said, but didn't.

'So what now?'

Shaking his head and trying to see the funny side, the older man said despairingly, 'God knows.' With his self-esteem low he turned on his heel and left abruptly, otherwise he'd have been there for ever, crawling up and down. Conscious of defeat, at least – he told himself feebly, 'I've said it. And had the last word. Maybe Jimmy bloody Plant will take the hint and transplant himself.' It was a vain hope but you never knew. Renegades were not noted for sensitivity to others, only to themselves.

The next morning the outhouse was abandoned, giving Hopkin the chance to hope more strongly. Again he was ambivalent deep within, regretting things he hadn't said about writing they could have perhaps discussed to their mutual benefit. It was a surprise to him that he should have desire for such a thing. It wasn't the dead teacher stirring, but the cause they had in common. Writers, probably all artists, were lonely and suspicious creatures. They ought to support each other but rarely did. Those heartbreaking letters of van Gogh said it all. Again he remembered that only with Bill had he experienced such kinship, before it turned sour and foundered as his friend sank into permanent depression.

The following morning he heard sounds again, on his way out to greet the pigs. Not a pig in sight, but there was Jimmy rooting away unstoppably. Hopkin groaned under his breath, again failing to be honest with himself. Glancing in he had a shock, registering what at first he took to be someone completely new. Jimmy's long hair had vanished: no plaits. He was bullet-headed in the new brutalist fashion, not shaved to the bone like a soccer star but it was closer than the old-style crewcut. Now he leaned in with his cranium all grim purpose. Twisting round he looked glaring-eyed, bloodshot, tight-lipped, barely able to tolerate the interruption. Also new, unless gone unnoticed, was a small brass ear-ring. Why only one? Hopkin had never understood the significance – as if it mattered.

When Jimmy spoke it softened the warrior appearance – a sort of joke. 'Sod it, was I humming again? Sorry, mate.'

'Did you come yesterday?' Hopkin enquired falsely, knowing full well he hadn't.

Jimmy shook his head in disgust. 'Couldn't crawl out of me pit. Maybe because of a girl in it with me. Till I kicked her out.' He added, 'Late night the night before. Crack party.'

His interviewer stared aghast. 'You do drugs?'

'Who wants to know?'

'I just thought – '

'If I wanted to I would, but I got no inclination to blot out. Not with this work to do.'

'I thought New Agers kept clear of drugs?'

'Who mentioned them? I'm talking about a few friends in town I used to hang out with. They do drugs now and then, that's their bag. No skin off my nose. Life's short, they're out to make it shorter. Up to them.'

'I'm not arguing.'

'Right.'

Hopkin felt unwanted. Smarting inwardly he said, 'I'll leave you to it.'

'Hang about.' Jimmy Plant had been screwing round his head. Now he manoeuvred himself into a position to face his uncertain host, as if to give extra weight to his words.

'What is it?'

'You mentioned the other day or whenever it was, on the lines of having sympathy for me.'

The baulked poet said, 'That's right,' though the context eluded him.

'No offence, Mister, but you can stuff your sympathy.' The rejection was uttered in a neutral tone.

'Is that it?'

Eyes in the white face suddenly glared. 'And don't fucking patronise me.'

'If that's what it sounded like I'm sorry.'

'Thought I'd mention it.'

'Is that all?'

'Nearly. The same goes for that half-cock advice you were trotting out on the subject of publishers and their likes and dislikes. Stuff that an' all.'

'I feel the same about advice. Or would do, if anybody offered me any concerning my own stuff. On other things, yes. I never listened. To tell the truth I'm inclined to be secretive when I'm on with something.'

'Interesting,' Jimmy said, clearly not interested.

'That it?'

As if he wasn't listening, Jimmy went on pursuing his quarry. 'You've probably heard of co-operatives, writer and reader joining forces and suchlike. It's in Writers and Artists or some reference tome. I'll investigate something of that nature when I've got things to show. When I'm good and ready.'

'Why not?'

'Didn't I say to stop patronising me?'

'Believe me I'm not.'

'Listen to yourself sometime, Hopkin.'

Chapter Fourteen

Another day, recorded as extraordinary in Hopkin's journal, was made so by the dissident novelist suddenly becoming expansive without warning. Was their relationship shifting from antagonistic to friendly? Hopkin had unearthed an Aladdin paraffin heater, and took it round to see if it could be put to use. This grey-green metal column, on its top a circular perforated plate you could stand a kettle or saucepan on, was an item he had carted in with the rest of his basic possessions and then forgotten. He had brought it with him thinking he might need it, and for nostalgic reasons. When he was newly married, poor, he had installed it in a box room and would position himself near it on winter days, backing up against it absent-mindedly with a book in his hand, or the typescript of something he was working on, scorching slits in his cord trousers with the heat. What had made him buy it was a photo he had seen once of Augustus John standing near an identical one, his mad eyes bulging. It appealed to him because it looked business-like, and for some reason nautical. The little ship of his poetry became linked in his other life with this steadfastly burning oil stove of his memory.

'I'm going to tell you something you might like to turn over,' the uptight young zealot announced, facing his fellow writer and even standing up, so that his average height was plain for all to see.

'Turn over?'

'In your head, man. Tell me what you think.'

The youngster's hands hung, raw and impatient-looking, with bitten nails, fingers plucking at his jeans, out at the knees as if the energy crackling through them had forced an exit for itself. He had no spare fat but was deep in the chest, unlike his narrow-chested listener. Hopkin was astonished at being addressed civilly for once, after being told only the day before to 'get real', whatever that meant. Nevertheless he was being made to wait, wondering as he submitted how masochistic he really was, if it was that or greedy curiosity which kept him from hitting out. He knew only too well that he had a tongue that could sting, 'a viper's tongue' his mother-in-law had once said.

'I'm all ears,' he said, risking a smile.

'They don't stick out that much,' Jimmy mocked.

His crypto-friend, if that was what he was, growing restive and nervous in the dead silence in which he lost touch with the other man completely, said as lightly as he could that the suspense was killing him.

Jimmy sat himself down again, letting his head droop as if studying the earth floor. 'I can tell you exactly what started me off on this game,' he said to his filthy trainers, glancing up sharp-eyed now and then as he went on. 'I was in this library, turning over one book after another till I was sick of print, and I came on this *Confessions of a Rebel*, Jack Clemo. You'll appreciate the title was right up my street, though I took it out without expecting much. Dipping in, it seemed full of religious crap and I was soon on the point of jacking it in. I stayed with it though. All at once it wouldn't let go, had me by the balls, this account of a kid growing up in some dreary shithole of a spot in Cornwall that was all clay dumps, these weird mountain cones sticking up wherever you looked. Dead land. I kept on, read about his illiterate parents and him half blind, deaf, everything stacked against him, all the same his mother had faith in something he wanted to do. Nothing stopped the poor bastard. Can you wonder I went overboard for this tale of woe? No? Wait till you hear my story, you'll see why.'

'I'll look forward to it.'

'Not my writin', me.'

'Yes, but I thought – '

'Heard of this Clemo?'

'Oh yes, certainly. I know his poetry but that's all.'

'Any good?'

'It's authentic, just as you say about his book. Belongs to no one, owes nothing to anybody. So true it hurts. The philosophy behind it repels me, that's all. The Calvinism.'

'But it's good? Real?'
'Definitely.'
'Try this *Confession* thing of his.'
'I will, now.'
'Might help. You look as if you could do with a shot in the arm.'
'Thanks.'
'No offence.'
'None taken.'
'All I'm sayin' is, so many books they call good send a bad smell up my nose.'
'Couldn't agree more.'

Even before Jimmy tore through an abbreviated version of his short unhappy life story he was touched by the unexpected show of trust. He wondered if bringing the Aladdin stove around had anything to do with it. Though he hadn't been allowed a glimpse of Jimmy's prose he was saddened to think of grievous disappointments in store for him when he tried to get a hearing for it. The barrier against it in his mind loomed so high that he was battering against it with bloody fists already, Hopkin thought, long before he should be bothering his head with such matters. Writing something that had shape and had a voice of your own was hard enough God knows, without creating more hardship for yourself.

Jimmy's face looked grim as he compared Clemo's devoted slum mother with his own. He hated his, his voice cold and venomous, he hoped she was dead wherever she was. It was a hackneyed story but still aroused Hopkin's pity, since here was the victim relating it. The father had pissed off, Jimmy said, when he and his sister were small. The man was rubbish. What happened next was so familiar from newspapers that Hopkin guessed right before he heard the rest. A moronic fat stepfather who had moved in took a belt regularly to Jimmy and abused his sister, whom he could hear begging for mercy, while the mother lay drunk and stinking in bed.

By early teenage Jimmy was hanging around with bad company, on drugs, looking for trouble, into petty crime. One night he had a fight with the stepfather and his mother kicked him out, screaming at him to get lost. His sister was on the game.

'That's what I mean,' Jimmy finished, 'when I say I got things to write about, real things, that nobody knows about but me.'

'You mean your own history, your feelings?'

But Hopkin had misjudged him badly, undervalued his intelligence. He regretted it instantly, too late, biting his lip.

'You think I don't know that what happened to me has been done to death in print?'

'I hoped you'd say that.' It was feeble and Hopkin knew it.

'Say what? I haven't said it yet. When I say real I mean out in the world real. Everybody lies in their teeth, from politicians down, think I don't know that? It's not the details of my fucked-up life so far that's important, it's what I feel, what I do, that's where the truth's hiding out. Getting at it, including the rage and hate, could make a book that blows up in their fat oily faces. That's what I'm tryin' for. In nobody's language but mine.'

'You probably don't need me to say so,' Hopkin said, as if on tiptoe, 'but I sincerely hope you achieve what you've set out to do.'

'Call me by my name. Jimmy's my name.'

'I'll remember,' the older man said self-consciously, unable to respond to order.

'What's your first again?'

'Matthew.'

Jimmy eyed him up and down curiously without speaking, until the other, nerves fraying, asked what was wrong.

'You're so edgy, man. I was going to say that since you're in love with titles you might like to know mine for this book when it's in the bag.'

Hopkin, surprised and flattered, said, 'You've got one?'

'I'm callin' it "Out Here Now". Go on, ask me why.'

'I think I know.'

'That's funny, since it's not clear to me yet. Except the obvious thing. What does it say to you?'

'Let me think about it.'

'I'll tell you what it says. Here's something bigger than all you arseholes and the little world you've made put together.'

'Never mind them, whoever they are. Let's hope it fulfils your expectations.'

Jimmy said irritably, 'Why are you always harping on hope? Don't you think I've got it in me, is that what you're sayin', behind your hope? In other words, do you have doubts about me as a writer? If you do, give it to me straight, don't wrap it up in hope this and hope that. You won't see me fall down and start howlin'. I'm more likely to spit in your eye.'

Hopkin, who had given up and was going, called back, 'If I've said it wrong again, excuse me. But there's no way I can answer your question before I've read a word.' He told himself that here was someone with a chip on his shoulder the size of one of those logs his backside was parked on.

He carried inside with him a warm feeling for all that. Wanting to respond symbolically, to demonstrate his own trust, he dug out a pamphlet of his poems, years old, published by a small press in the north, and took it back to the outhouse. To Jimmy's concentrated back he said, 'Here's a bit of my own stuff you might like to glance at sometime. I'd like to know what you think. Sorry to interrupt.' Dropping it on the table-door he dodged out again, quick.

Settling down at his own workplace he wound a fresh sheet into the machine and then opened his file, wondering if he felt the same. A shiver ran down his spine as he read at speed. His 'Missing Life' embryo was alive and kicking in spite of these major interruptions. Yesterday he had confronted dead words, his heart failing. Now, by some alchemy outside his control, it had regained its promise. He tapped out the word

    Lena

as if inviting her ghost to come, to enter him. Then he ran full tilt at poem number three:

> This is a letter
> for the night's delivery.
> The little train on its fixed track
> led you north,
> bending comically to the left
> and then out of sight,
> a caterpillar made of tin.

Black Rainbow

The bathroom tap has stopped dripping.
You are missing from the space
between chairs:
the house and its walls
listen for you.
Your going away returns me
to the point
where my existence changed course.

There is just the heat
weighing on my head, on the plants
we have watered, everything.
The sun treats us equally
on its great arc,
pouring life unstoppably,
even for those who can't live,
who can't bear to be reminded
of how magnificent the world
once was. Beauty on earth.
In this blinding light.

Chapter Fifteen

Jimmy Plant handed him the pamphlet the very next day. He braced himself for the worst.

'I got it wrong about you. Straight up, mate, I did. That one, what was it, "Born Unborn", it really hit me where I live. Swung me up and away, sweet as jazz. I admit it, I took you for just a teacher who has to keeping sticking the dead past on people. You're all right. Not my language but everybody to their own. Yours rings right to me, that's all I care about. I can feel the heart and guts.'

'Thank you.'

'Now you think you're hot shit.'

'No. All I hope is that what I'm on with now is what you call the real thing.'

'Stop hoping and do it.'

Now he had successfully reversed their roles, Jimmy sealed his advice with a twisted grin. Laughed Hopkin, 'Is that your advice?'

'It's mine to me.'

He turned his back, which Hopkin saw now as comradely, if embarrassed to be so. He went off and made coffee for them both, putting the mug down beside the writing hand and smiling to himself at the grunt of acknowledgement.

There had been a scare, when Michael dropped in to ask if Hopkin had been troubled by mice, since the previous long-stay tenant had once lodged a complaint. The conversation went on with the half-born poet in an agony of uncertainty, not knowing whether Jimmy was still in residence. He answered from a tight throat that no, he hadn't seen any, and in fact would welcome some company, a joke that misfired because Mrs Symonds, it seemed, felt herself morally bound to clear the cottage of vermin. His father would come down shortly, Michael promised, to block up any holes he could find.

Should Hopkin invite Jimmy into the cottage proper for his morning sessions? If he did that, how could he pass him off to the owners? All this was assuming Jimmy agreed to come in out of the cold. He vacillated wildly, torn between a need to preserve his own privacy, a desire to feel well of himself and a fear of being exposed as a harbourer of human flotsam or accused of homosexuality. Then he was given another fright.

'I need to take a leaf out of your book and use a typer,' Jimmy remarked out of the blue. Hopkin went cold as he heard. 'It would sharpen some of this up, I might see the wood for the trees.' Noticing the other's tense face he said, grinning, 'Stop shitting yourself, I shan't bring it here. I used to borrow the one belonging to my girl, Kath, only we seem to be about to split. Not only was it getting too heavy, it's gone from honey to poison all of a sudden, know what I mean? Though I owe her a lot, she's been great for me in all departments, not least in bed. If I got a few drinks down her she'd ride me like a horse, then fall off pissing herself when I yelled 'Tally-ho.' That was a long time ago. She's stopped laughing and stopped pretending. Women pretend a lot, do you find that yourself?'

'Pretend?'

'They're in to pleasing you, only what they're really after Christ knows. Either they want kids or they're into some secret agenda you're not party to. Or ever likely to be. That so in your experience?'

Hopkin said it was an interesting theory and he'd think about it. It was oddly similar to the notions he'd been trotting out to Marianne's housemate, when he considered later. What disturbed him afterwards as a result of this conversation was the sudden renewal in him of sexual longing, which he thought was long dead. His wife's death had spiritualised him, and this stirring of heat dismayed and shamed him in the grieving part of himself. It soon died, and he forgot how it had briefly tormented him.

One Saturday he was in Stroud, feeling too tired to hike back and moving fast from the library to catch one of the rare buses to Ash.

There on the pavement approaching was Jimmy Plant, hooked by the arm to a woman, presumably his 'girl'. His hands were in his pockets and he looked sullen, if submissive. Seeing Hopkin he seemed more caught than ever, as if he would have liked to jump over a roof and disappear. The woman, nearly old enough to be his mother, was slight, dark-haired, walking with a loping stride to match the young man she held firmly, gazing sideways at him with intelligent amusement. Her trench coat was stone-coloured, spotless, her companion as slovenly as ever. As they drew level with him, Hopkin felt sure she was perfectly aware of what an incongruous couple they made. He had no grounds for thinking it, except for an ironic smile as she was introduced to him. Jimmy grimaced, as if a bad smell had wafted up his nostrils.

They were shaking hands, the woman allowing hers to lie negligent in his. He was reminded of an African he knew once who greeted him as bonelessly. Her feminine touch spoke to him sadly of a world from which he had been banished.

'I've heard about you,' she said. He was struck by the pallor of her creamy skin. 'You're the poet, right?'

Her voice was light and pleasant. He laughed, his turn to look abashed, searching in her eyes for mockery but there was none.

'Nothing so grand,' he said. 'Poets who are that and nothing else are like priests to me, or should be.'

'I think I know what you mean,' Katherine said.

Jimmy, squirming disagreement and ill at ease, Hopkin thought, in a busy street exchanging chit-chat instead of at his task, invited his fellow writer to a birthday party the following Saturday at Katherine's place. 'Unless you got better things to do like.'

'Who's going?' Hopkin asked warily.

'Rob and his girl, and us two.'

'Yes, come,' the woman said.

'Whose birthday is it?'

'Mine,' she said. She pulled a sour mouth, cancelling it with a laugh.

Alone again, he told himself in alarm that he'd never liked parties, felt a clown at them, exposed, a fish out of water. He had turned up before at gatherings, expecting an intimate few, only to find a heaving crowd. Moreover, he was now a solitary, seen by some as almost a recluse. Small talk, always difficult for him, had become virtually impossible. It was Katherine's warm invitation that had made him feel less of a hermit at bay than he believed he was. He spent a week unable to decide and then found himself tramping down the drive heading for Ash in the early evening of another Saturday, in his duffle bag a bottle of red wine.

What was pulling him, reeling him in? Was it loneliness, which he'd thought he'd conquered? Or could it be a buried, unacknowledged desire for female company? The involuntary physical flow of current in his groin had not recurred. He saw himself as maimed as far as women were concerned. Lena had held his life between her two hands and he hadn't fallen out, nor would he ever, not now. Death had sealed their union as even life couldn't do. His stride quickening, he thought he was probably just starved for company in general: foolish but excusable. If it followed the pattern of the few parties he had suffered he would be cursing himself for an idiot before an hour had gone. In Ash he went to the one place where he had seen a taxi waiting, and there it was.

Katherine, he discovered, lived in a flat two flights up over a delicatessen. You went up bleak uncarpeted stairs and entered another world, rosily lit, with low sloping ceilings, the windows under the eaves. These were attic rooms. Bare varnished boards were half covered with Indian rugs in deep purples and bloody reds. Only Jimmy's pal Rob was there with his girl Tess. Not knowing them he was at a loss. They were coiled around each other on a sofa. Sinuous jazz came from somewhere, the sax playing over a double bass and drum with such eloquence and invention that he asked what it was: it was something to say.

'Andy Sheppard,' Rob said, his voice thick with drink.

The name meant nothing to him. Coming in he had passed a heavily pregnant woman in the street, her belly flowering. Under the influence of this music improvising so effortlessly he flowered in his own belly, greatly surprised to find himself still sensuously alive. The sax playing was virtuoso stuff, squeaking off the scale, emitting low growls, singing high and sweet, all along a path that the double bass was beating in a subtle and beautiful duet.

Katherine and Jimmy came in: they had been shopping for food and drink. He felt awkward before them, an old misfit in young company, trying to see her in her middle age as a bridge between them. She seemed to accept him for what he was, and so, he had to admit, did they. As always his problem was with himself.

'I didn't think you'd come,' Katherine cried, he thought happily.

'Neither did I,' he confessed. She was bustling into the kitchen and perhaps didn't hear. It sounded discourteous, though he had meant to joke. He told himself ruefully that jokes always misfired on him. Jimmy Plant seemed to be studiously ignoring him, his eyes unsure, which was funny he thought in such a small space. But he knew his ways now well enough not to be bothered.

Rob – he didn't catch the surname – impressed him not at all: a goon of a character with yellowish gap teeth and a beard that was thin and straggled weakly, refusing to grow dense. Hair the same, down on his shoulders in thin stringy bunches. He failed to understand the basis of the friendship with Jimmy, bright as a button by contrast for all his acting the savage. Tess sat on Rob's lap looking bored, legs gaping in the smallest of bright yellow minis, saved from total exposure by bottle-green tights, black panties. She was brighter than she looked, he imagined. Her gaze followed Jimmy about, though he seemed oblivious. He was looking cleaner than Hopkin had ever seen him, in a white roll-top cotton sweater and jeans that were worn but in one piece.

Katherine came in with a tray of cheesy titbits, bowls of peanuts and crisps. Her startlingly plain black dress down to her ankles, scooped at the neck, gave Hopkin a real surprise. He had taken her for slim and here she was in the flesh looking bountiful and admitting it. She moved with the grace of someone who had always been feline, weight or no weight.

He was expecting others to arrive, but no one did. The wine flowed. Someone changed the tape to rock, the volume too high, making conversation a strain. How had he been included in such an intimate group? Within an hour he was staring with blurred vision at the scraggy top of Rob's head as it sagged forward between his knees. His useless arms hung down. Jimmy disappeared and then there was the clackety-clack of a typewriter. Hopkin looked enquiringly at Katherine and she laughed bitterly, he thought. 'He's in my bedroom, at that sodding book,' she said, shrugging. Leaning over she whispered, 'See who keeps him company.'

Sure enough, in a few minutes Tessa slipped out of the room.

'She's a friendly soul,' Katherine said, heavily sarcastic. 'But look at this piss artist. Can you blame her?'

Hopkin asked, 'Is it ended between you and Jimmy? He hinted as much to me.'

She sat down on the floor in front of him. 'Did he now? The short answer's yes. Can I use you for a back rest?'

He said she was welcome.

She rested her spine against his legs, telling him she was tired suddenly after a busy week as a dentist's receptionist.

'Is it boring?'

'Fairly. They're nice people to work for.'

He heard her voice slurring a little. Rob hung motionless as if frozen in his grotesque drooping fall.

'Is he asleep?'

'Out like a light. Always happens.'

Jimmy came back in, his expression vague, followed by Tess after a decent interval.

They sat in silence. The music stopped playing. Hopkin felt extraordinarily peaceful and at one with life. Katherine reached up for his hands, which rested quietly on his knees, placing one on her throat. When he sat in a commotion, making no move, she pushed his hands away.

'My mistake. I do stupid things when I drink.'

He couldn't bring himself to speak.

Over in the corner Tess was doing her best to interest Jimmy, who sat in a slump with his face averted, studying the ceiling.

Hopkin, saying goodnight near midnight, couldn't get Katherine to meet his gaze. He left in confusion. He suspected her action as a form of retaliation against Jimmy, nothing to do with him. He was glad to escape the company of the raw young, walking blind with his jabbering thoughts along dark country roads.

Monday morning saw Hopkin's unofficial, half welcome, half

unwanted guest hard at work as usual, not even lifting his head when he was brought a mug of hot tea. On a bleak morning the Aladdin stove stood unlit, though it contained a gallon of fuel. Hopkin thought he had perhaps only presented it as a sop to his conscience. When Jimmy did deign to speak he made no reference to the so-called party. The same went for succeeding days.

Suddenly he stopped coming. As one morning followed another, Hopkin was at first relieved, then regretful at the thought of no more discussion, abortive or otherwise. Really he was left feeling lonely, whereas before Jimmy's intrusion he had been living proudly and well in a state of growing self-sufficiency, something he had never achieved before.

What had begun as unwelcome had left him wanting to be intruded upon. He cursed Jimmy Plant for overturning his stability, leaving him restless and pathetically in need of – what? Finally he was nagged by a voice telling him to find out what had happened. Next time he was in Ash he'd get into a call box and ring Katherine, who would surely know.

He did so on his next shopping trip, and got her answering machine. He put down the phone, frustrated, before the end of the message. He remembered about her job at the dentist's, so maybe she stayed there for lunch. He toyed with the idea of calling her at work, but wasn't sure where that was, and it seemed a bad idea. Nor could he bring himself to ask for the use of Symonds' phone. He marched down the road one evening early in the rainy dark and rang again from the village. This time she was there.

'This is Matthew Hopkin, if you remember me.'

'Hello,' she answered, in a voice suggesting she did, but only just.

'Excuse me for bothering you,' he faltered.

'What is it?'

'It's only that I was wondering if you had any news of Jimmy.'

'News?'

'You know he'd got into the habit of parking himself here while he was writing his book.'

As he gabbled this into the vacuum he lost track of his motives for asking. What was this saying about himself?

'Yes, of course. That's how you met.'
'That's right.'
'What about it?'
'He doesn't come any more.'
'I'm not surprised.'
'Why's that?'

Feeling more absurd than ever, wishing he'd not made this stupid call, he hung in the void and waited to be set free. When she spoke again she had a different, welcoming voice, the one he remembered hearing when they first met. 'I'll tell you later,' she said, and chuckled. 'Let's see, how about Saturday? Come round for lunch. Can you manage that?'

'It's very good of you.'
'What kind of things do you eat? Would a risotto do?'
'It would. But please don't put yourself to any trouble.'

She laughed, a rich sound. 'People always say that. Why is it trouble if you want to do it?'

He agreed gladly: the English at their worst, never saying what they mean. He asked when he should come, and she told him any time after noon.

For the rest of the week, struggling to recapture old ground he had occupied and lived in productively – though how easily it had been overrun – he thought of the hole left by Jimmy's absence, of his own isolation, of the coming meeting and lunch with Katherine in her hospitable flat. Why was he looking forward to Saturday with such zest? Was he as vulnerable and desperate as all that? He didn't think so, yet here he was eager to break out. He had read somewhere once – in Doctor Zhivago? – that unshared happiness was not happiness. By the same token, he reasoned, an unshared meal was not a meal, unshared writing was not writing, an unshared life a mockery of a life. Had he been deceiving himself through these months when he had thought he was being courageous? He had lost faith in all he had gained in his solitary hours, and had room in his heart for nothing more than one lunch with a woman he scarcely knew. Human contact was all it amounted to, he told himself in an access of self-pity. He attacked a new poem in too gloomy a spirit and it foundered almost at once.

Chapter Sixteen

He could smell something cooking as soon as he entered the little top floor flat, which looked entirely different in daylight, so that he was bewildered. Also, Katherine Wells didn't match with his remembrance of her for some reason. What was it? She wore leggings, black; a long white top with coloured stitching around the neckline. Her hair was gathered up in a style different from the time before. Sunlight was hitting the window facing the street and she pulled down a beige linen blind.

'Take the weight off your feet,' she said. He sat down obediently.

There was an oval table, already laid with a crisp blue cloth, place settings for two, wine glasses. When he got up again to ask if he could help she suggested he open the bottle of white wine in the fridge.

'I should have brought something,' he said.

'Why, isn't this enough?'

'Yes, of course. I'll return the compliment one day. But I'm a primitive cook. You might get lentil soup and a mushroom omelette on a good day.'

'Nothing wrong with that.'

At the table, spooning a helping on to his plate, she said why didn't he make this for himself, it was so simple. 'It's something you can do all in once saucepan.'

'Now I'm interested.'

'Saute the onions and mushrooms in a little oil, add the rice, some stock, not too much because the can of tomatoes provides plenty of liquid, garlic if you like that, last of all the tuna about ten minutes before you're ready to eat. Isn't that easy?'

'Even I could cope with that.'

Throughout the meal they had avoided the subject of Jimmy. Over the coffee, noticing her waist cinched with a broad shiny black belt, her hips swelling within the black hug of her leggings, he got over his initial shyness and met her blunt gaze directly.

'Obviously you know something I don't,' he said.

'I can't tell you where Jimmy's gone but I can guess,' she said tonelessly. 'And I can guess who with.'

'So he's not around here any more?'

'This flat?'

'I meant Stroud,' he said, embarrassed. 'To tell you the truth I don't know why I'm asking.'

She shook her head, smiling grimly at thoughts of her own. 'Gone to London is my guess. He talked about it often enough. How it was the only place to be if you were going to make it as a writer. He was ready to spit on the literary scene but had to get amongst it all the same, because according to what he'd sussed out it was there or nowhere.' She added, stirring in vinegar, 'And you can bet little Tessa is with him. She's got friends there who can put him up, she said. And she won't be going along with his book dreams for long like I did, waiting for him to notice her when he needs a break from his toil.'

Listening intently, her guest was considering at the same time why this woman seemed admirable to him in spite of the bile. She had a natural way with her. All right, she was of a mature age, but it didn't follow from that necessarily. He imagined she had always been without coquetry, something he had always disliked about girls he had met and tried to befriend when he was young and single. They fluttered, widened their eyes, their voices small: he was soon on the run. His bashfulness disabled him so often that he had given up and blamed them, knowing it was him too. Then Lena came along, separated, with a child, and she dealt with him so capably that he was made to feel valued for the first time ever. He had loved her and wanted her from that time on.

This Katherine was he thought indifferent to anything about herself that might please a man. It didn't bother him: on the contrary. He felt himself a man apart, something he would be for a long time to come.

'He spoke well of you,' he ventured to say. 'He gave me the impression that he owed you a great deal.'

'You chewed me over between you?'

'No, nothing like that. It was just a comment he happened to make. About you being a boon.'

'You're telling me I was. Apart from money, the use of my typewriter, this quiet flat when he wanted to drop in here and commune with his muse, he got a hell of a lot of moral support from me.' She spoke hotly, as if still involved, out of some hurt he knew nothing about. He saw the difficult emotions on her face and groped for something to say next. She forestalled him. 'Go on, ask me,' she said. 'Were we lovers? Could he have fancied an old bird like me?'

He said, 'At my age I can't see you as anything but young.'

'Thanks.'

'I think Jimmy was fortunate having you for a friend or whatever,' he said lamely. 'He can't be the easiest of people. Though I hardly know him, this didn't stop him having a verbal swing at me more than once.'

She drew a deep breath. 'Jimmy has a mother problem.'

'Well, for reasons best known to himself he once gave me a potted version of his history. Do you mean a mother-hate problem?'

'Leaving aside the shitty things he's done to me, and now dropping me for that kid with her skirt hitched up round her arse, there was something about him that affected me, I admit it. What he was trying to do against the odds with his sodding book.'

'Did you read any of it?' he had to ask.

'Bits. What I could decipher through his horrible handwriting.' She laughed harshly. 'I got him using my typewriter so I could read it better.'

'I don't see you as that selfish, but go on.'

'About what?'

'His book.'

'I don't know what to say. Ungrammatical, plenty of gibberish, but one or two of the scenes were so awful, so true, I burst out crying once in front of him.'

'How did he react?'

'Furious, he was. Snatched it from me and ran off. I never found out why.'

She pulled back, became guarded, shooting him a glance that was almost a plea, so that he felt impelled to change the painful subject by saying abruptly, 'Have you been married? Excuse me for asking.'

She nodded, 'Does it show?'

'Not in a bad way.' He meant to go on; thought better of it.

'Once properly, once shacked up. I've got a son of eighteen.'

'Around here?'

'At college. Bristol.'

He thought it fitting to respond with a brief history of his own. She listened without interruption. 'That's dreadful,' she said. 'I'm sorry.'

Suddenly, with a sick wrench, he was putting his feelings on trial. Was he in mourning for himself? He wanted to confide in her, but it was too soon. Instead he asked after her son, and whether they were on good terms. She hadn't mentioned his name.

'Justin.'

'I've got a son of my own, married,' he explained. 'I'm a grandfather in fact.'

'Justin leads his own life,' she told him. 'He has his circle of friends, shares a student house with three others. I'll be lucky to see him at Easter. As for how we get on together, he's become steadily more critical of me. And he has dissatisfactions, the kind you get at his age. I have the feeling that sex worries him, what to do about it, if anything, which is fairly typical I think, in spite of the banging on about it they hear nonstop from all quarters. There's more pressure on the young now than ever if you ask me, far more than in my day. God, I don't envy them.'

'Less guilt?' he suggested.

'Guilt has its uses.'

'Does he see his father at all?'

'A little contact. Very sporadic. Mind you, he doesn't confide in me any more.'

'That's a shame. With your empathy you could perhaps help him.'

'My what?' She said mockingly, yet seemed pleased. 'I wish he *would* say things. His father would be useless though. Men are. Present company excluded.'

'Included would be more accurate. I can only express myself properly on paper.'

'Don't knock it.'

He responded readily. 'I don't. I write in a journal as a means of speaking to my wife, and now I'm writing poetry that might make a book, with the same end in view. Though I hope it'll lead out from the purely personal.' He stopped suddenly. 'Does that sound morbid to you?'

If she had said yes, and with her frank speaking she was more than capable, it would have made him clam up. But what she said surprised and pleased him no end. 'Not if it makes you a better person,' she said.

'I can hope.'

'As for me, I don't know what I am.'

'Did you think you did when you got married?'

'When you're that young you know everything, remember?'

'Dimly.'

'At least you know what you want to do. Even Jimmy knows that.' She suddenly laughed raucously. 'Even Jimmy!'

'Maybe knowing what you don't want is important too.'

'I'm no good at that either. My life is full of wrong choices.'

He took a chance and said, 'Does you son, Justin, does he know about Jimmy?'

She shook her head emphatically. 'No fear. He'd have hated me. Told me I was disgusting. Kids of that age can be horribly self-righteous.'

He agreed. 'I remember how I was. Insufferable.'

She sat musing. 'You're probably wondering how I got Jimmy to clear out when Justin came to stay. I simply told him straight. Expecting a real mouthful I can tell you. To my amazement he was almost considerate, didn't object at all. Made himself scarce and took a week coming back. I thought I'd seen the last of him. He can be sweet when he wants, believe it or not. Of course you have to watch out for his stupid pride.'

'Don't tell me.'

'My trouble is I can't wrap things up.'

'You sound two of a kind.'

She sat burrowing away at something inside herself. 'Do I strike you as the maternal type?'

'I hardly know you.'

'True.'

'Why do you ask?' he said, touched by her trust in him.

She was back in the recent past, he thought, judging by the faraway look. 'Maybe that's all I was to Jimmy, the mother he never had. It's an obvious conclusion to reach.'

'The son with a grudge?'

She shook her head. 'That wasn't how I saw him, not once.'

'Maybe you pitied rather than loved him.'

'Ask me another. How do you tell? Once I came across him crying and it really cut me up.'

'What was it about?'

She produced the same raucous laugh, and this time it jarred. 'His writing!' she shouted. 'He couldn't do it, he was stuck. That was his real mistress, that bloody book. Little Miss Tessa's got a lot to learn.'

Hopkin, sitting neatly at the edge of someone else's life, feeling privileged but also slightly ridiculous, had begun to wonder at his own ulterior motives. Was this talk about Jimmy Plant making him obscurely jealous? He thought not, then in the next breath asked a leading question. 'Would you say you're still committed to him in one sense?'

She reddened, denying it strongly. 'Is that how I sound?'

'I was only thinking aloud.'

'So am I, now. Why are you so curious about us?'

He sat asking himself. 'I suppose because he's such an unknown quantity to me.'

'You know how it is with a relationship. You give more than you should, then have to resign yourself to the missing part of yourself somebody's walked off with. If you see what I mean.'

'Breaking up must be hell. Not that I've experienced what you describe exactly.'

'Yours is even worse.'

'One day though you'll wake up and see the world through different eyes. You'll wonder what it was all about. Somebody said that to me once when I was sinking fast.'

'Who?'

'A doctor.'

She had stopped listening. Sounding furious with herself, mouth in a twist she let fly, at men in general he guessed. 'The trouble with being somebody's stand-in mother is that it gives them problems,' she said viciously.

'Does it?'

'In bed it does. Poking your mother is the last thing you want to be caught doing.'

He flushed and felt brief distaste. She added at once, 'Sorry. I told you I find it hard to wrap things up.'

'I was warned.'

'You're quite right, I'm not over the little shit, not yet. I will be, though.'

'I don't doubt it for a minute.'

He sat watching her anger subside. She caught him studying her. 'I wish I knew what you were thinking this minute,' she said. 'No, perhaps I don't.'

'Nothing clear enough to express.'

'A great help you are.'

'Sorry.'

'You're a deep one, I think.'

He shook his head. 'It's a fallacy. People think so because I'm quiet. I confess I've let them think that sometimes. The older I get, the more I'm conscious of mysteries in others that I'm outside, without a clue to what's going on inside them.'

'Can I ask you how old you are?'

He told her. 'I can't believe it but it's true.'

'You look younger.'

'So they say. I was in my forties before men stopped saying "son" to me.'

She laughed. 'When they start calling you dad, then you can worry.'

'I'll be past caring.'

He made an excuse and got up to go. 'I know, your writing,' She said, a trifle sourly. 'You've got to get back to it. Shades of Jimmy.'

To prove her wrong he sat down again. 'I know his feeling but you're wrong in my case. It's just that I don't want to intrude on your weekend.'

'It's funny the way I end up getting acquainted with creative people.'

'Was your husband one?'

'Yes. A creative liar.'

They both laughed. 'Well, you could see fiction as a kind of lying. Plays too. We say someone's acting, making it up.'

'Would you like a drink?'

He said yes, settling for whisky and dry ginger. She drank hers straight. Wanting to know her more, he asked, 'What music appeals to you?'

'Oh, Rachmaninov, Chopin. Not at the moment, I'm too weepy. I read instead. Wading through *Middlemarch* just now.' She laughed lightly. 'Don't be impressed, I like long reads.'

'You saw it on TV?'

'Yes. It gave me an urge to read all the parts they hadn't used.'

'Tell me what you like about it?'

She thought hard, frowning. 'Let's see. Well, the leisurely pace for one thing. And the – what's the word – the gravity. It slows me down, I like that. Also it makes me feel, how shall I say, significant, don't ask me why.' She thought again. 'Sometimes I read those fat books by Iris Murdoch for the same reason. Then at the end I'm left wondering what it was all about.'

'It was about making you feel significant.'

'Serves me right when I find I'm not.'

'You're too hard on yourself.'

'I'm a dull person.'

'No.'

'I *feel* dull.'

'It's winter,' he said. 'You're hibernating, like me.'

He got up finally with determination, asking before he left if he could look at the view through the window. 'Glad to oblige,' she said, and raised the blind. The sun had shifted. He gazed out over the low roofs opposite and saw willows in the distance, which he thought could be the river. They shook hands formally and he said, 'This is what everyone says but in my case it's the truth. I've enjoyed it very much, food and drink and the company.'

'Good.'

He wondered if she would care to visit him sometime, joking that he'd be glad to show her round his estate. She said she'd like that. He suggested Boxing Day. 'Unless you do something traditional?'

'Nothing like that.'

'Come and sing carols with me.'

'You haven't heard my singing. I can't hold a tune.'

'We'll be off-key together.'

On Christmas Eve afternoon he was called to the farm phone. Her voice, sounding happy, told him she was sorry but she'd have to come over another time. 'My wayward son's come breezing in, complete with Christmas tree and a turkey.'

'That's wonderful. Has he struck it rich?'

'Student loan. Which makes him deeper in debt than ever.'

'So I'll see you later.'

'I'll be in touch, shall I?'

'Please do.'

He wished them both a merry Christmas. Persuading himself that it was nothing, nursing a secret disappointment, he turned to leave and was asked by Symonds to come down that evening for mince pies and a glass of something. In normal circumstances he would have declined with thanks.

'Thank you, I will,' he said, with gratitude in his heart.

Chapter Seventeen

His mother was expecting him for New Year's Eve. He had always welcomed the turn of the year, and the sense of a clean slate before him. He would rather have stayed put, but had promised. When he was away from her, the image of his mother, sentenced to endless empty time, waiting hopelessly to rejoin her husband of fifty-six years, was somehow worse than the reality. Hopkin's heart would sink when he drew near, though he knew she had her good moments and consoled herself with them.

She did her best to enter into the spirit of the occasion for her son, but her forlorn face when she thought she was unobserved pierced him through. Her simple religious faith had failed her. Why had she been smashed to the ground by a death like a thunderbolt, striking her husband down in minutes as they were about to set off for the coast on a day trip, innocent as children? This wasn't her, it was him being her, taking her fits of dejection as the whole of her life. Yet it was true that she peered from her cottage window at an enchanting view that now mocked her, without a husband to share it. She had said to Hopkin in a fit of weeping that she didn't want to go on, the world more and more terrified her, changing always for the worse on her TV screen. Now here she was being festive, the Christmas decorations still in place. He was ashamed to find himself counting the hours. He could do nothing, say nothing for her.

Had she enjoyed her time with his sister over Christmas?

'June's very good. She always makes me welcome.'

'Why shouldn't she?'

'Adrian puts up with me.'

'You always say that.'

'When he comes for me in the car he hardly speaks. It's like sitting with a taxi driver.'

'Offer him a tip,' he joked.

'It's true.'

Adrian was his sister's second husband. 'I wouldn't call him a warm person,' he said to his mother. 'But how would I know?'

'He isn't!'

'Some people just find it hard to say things.'

'He does.'

'I'm sure he means well.'

'He's never once said my name.'

'Give him time,' he tried to joke. 'He's only known you ten years.'

'My name's Maud, I said to him once.'

'What did he say?'

'Nothing!'

In her darkest moments she would now and then turn on her son spitefully. 'Where are you now?' she asked once.

'I don't follow you.'

'You aren't here, you're miles away. Where are you?'

'Don't be funny.'

'It's true.'

'What's wrong?'

'I feel just as lonely as when I'm on my own.'

Upset, he said he was sorry. 'I was working on a poem in my head,' he excused himself. 'In cloud-cuckoo land you'd call it.'

She was instantly remorseful, on the point of tears. 'Take no notice, I don't mean it. I'm a horrible old woman.'

'No, no, you mustn't say that. You're all sorts of things, not any one thing.'

'Men are nicer than women, if they're nice that is.'

'Sounds Irish.'

'I've never met a woman as nice as your father was.'

'I'm sure he'd have said the same about you.'

'No he wouldn't!'

'All right, you're terrible,' he said.

'Sons are nicer than daughters.'

'Shall I make us a milk drink?'

'Yes, please,' she said docilely, like a child.

Standing beside her patiently, he thought then that like Katherine and himself, his mother was a sad creature in limbo.

She came in an old blue Metro which he didn't know she possessed, stepping forth in a long woolly coat, dark, a crimson scarf wound round her neck. Hatless. The day was overcast, the wind clattering and cold. He had hoped for sun but this was typical of most of his winter days. 'Where are your gloves?' he asked her, and she told him not to fuss, she had pockets.

He took her past the high stone cliff of the big farmhouse, wanting her to marvel at it, which she did. 'It's so grand,' she said, goggling.

'Inside it's more like Bleak House. Not that anyone seems to mind. They're a tough breed, farmers.'

He caught a glimpse of Michael hurrying between two farm buildings. By the time he came to point him out he'd disappeared. He did draw her attention to one or two animals, a cow and two bullocks, and said they all had names. She didn't find it quaint. 'It's what I'd do,' she said, 'if I were an animal person, which I suppose I'm not.'

Back in the cottage he showed her round, even mentioning on the stairs the lean-to Jimmy had squashed himself into. 'Aren't you curious?' he asked, then regretted his lack of tact.

She made nothing of it. 'No,' was all she said.

He had invited her to tea and had bought scones, uncut and waiting under a dish in the kitchen. 'Terribly English,' he said.

'Lovely, It's something I never have these days. I'll be reminded of my aunties.'

'So that's who I remind you of.'

'Not exactly. You *are* a fusser though, I can see that.'

Upstairs he showed her the bedrooms, two: his with the unmade double bed. Down in the bare sitting room he had built a wood fire, crackling cheerfully behind a fireguard, but up here the atmosphere was chilly, damp. She shivered involuntarily. Inspired by her presence, her female receptiveness, he was tempted to leave his seclusion and suggest crawling into bed, to exchange body heat if nothing else, but his desire, such as it was, was undercut by his wife's palpable reality, not only in the journal he had already shown Katherine but everywhere.

Spirit of the Woods

He found it hard to say whether she could read his thoughts. She went ahead of him quickly to the stairs and down.

'I forgot to ask if you like tea,' he said.

'If you have scones it's got to be tea.'

'You're right.'

He went to make tea and she followed him to the kitchen. He asked after her Christmas with the son who'd come bearing gifts. 'Did he stay long?'

'He was off again Boxing Day morning. I could have come anyway.'

'But it went well?'

She pulled a face. 'It always does for the first few hours. Then Justin comes out with something – or I do – and before you know it we're saying things we wish afterwards we hadn't. Well, I regret it. I can't speak for him.'

'You get on each other's nerves.'

'Every time. Sometimes I really think he hates me.'

'But he came.'

'He came.'

She buttered the scones. He showed her where to find the blackcurrent conserve.

Afterwards they sat in silence, as if the very place discouraged talk. He asked, 'Too quiet for you?'

'You must be joking. I love it.'

He was grateful, looking at her warmly with appreciation, even though underneath there was a grain of resentment. There had been no other woman here but Lena's ghost until now. By some curious twist or wriggle he saw her as a transgressor, regardless of the fact that he'd invited her.

She gazed into the fire. He threw on another log. A half consumed log shifted its weight, sending up a shower of sparks. Speaking to her and also to himself, to the room, the silence, he said, 'How do you see the future?'

She laughed throatily but looked uneasy. 'Me? I can never see beyond the end of my nose.'

'My future's dwindling, I feel mortal, yet I still look ahead when the spirit moves me. I suppose while you're alive, you live.'

'I imagine so.'

'So you go on from day to day?'

'I wish I did. It's the wisest way to live, surely.'

'If you can manage it.'

'Exactly.'

Neither of them spoke for a while, then they both began at once. 'Go on,' he said.

'I admit I'm unhappy with my life so far. So many stupid mistakes, climbing into bed with someone out of anxiety, needing to be needed, wasting time with unpredictable characters like Jimmy, who gives more to his obsession than he could ever give to me. I'm old enough to know better but I'm not better. I'm stupid.'

He asked if she would like a drink. He had bought brandy: the words 'brandy for courage' had stuck in his head. She said no, involved in her self-examination.

'I like surprises,' she went on, 'that's why Justin turning up out of the blue was lovely. Perhaps that's why I land up in messes. Jimmy was one surprise too many.'

'At least he has the guts to be himself, whatever that means.'

'Yes, that attracted me. No bullshit in him.'

He thought for a moment, hesitated, then said, 'If Jimmy turned up on your doorstep tomorrow, what would you do?'

She looked troubled. 'Do? I realise what I *should* do if I've got a grain of sense, but would I?' She shook her head passionately, like a girl. 'I've seen the last of him, it's hypothetical. Isn't it about time I called you by your name?'

'Please do.'

'Here's a question for you, Matthew. Time you wrestled with one.'

'I often do, but they're my own.'

'How long do you expect to stay holed up here writing to your dead wife? Forgive me for being crude.'

'It's a good question. You're not the first to ask it. I can only say as long as it takes. No answer but it's the best I can do.'

'You give me the impression of someone waiting for something to happen.'

'If I am, it's out there,' he said, pointing out of the window.

'Come again?'

'The springtime. I'm waiting for spring.'

'Then what?'

'I'll tell you when it happens.'

She gave a snort of impatience. 'Writers are never straightforward. Are you talking about something inside you that's going to spring out, you hope?'

'I don't know what I'm talking about.' He was afraid now of losing touch with a nameless force, that he'd so glibly named.

She was observing him bleakly. 'You're a good listener. I hope I am. I find it easy to tell you things. You don't know what a compliment it is to a woman when she feels she's really being listened to. Jimmy listened, but he was such a child. No wonder he needed a mother. My husband was a man who was such a liar, you didn't know how many times he'd cheated. Not Jimmy, I could see right through him. Perhaps that's what he ran away from.'

'Aren't all men children as far as women are concerned?'

'You are and you aren't, I can't decide.'

'Anyway, I hope we can be friends,' he said, suddenly very moved by her.

'Oh I hope so. We already are, aren't we?'

'Yes, it's happened,' he said, rather stiffly.

The oddness of his remark caused her to stare, as if seeing him for the first time. 'You're a strange man.'

Something about him, or about them both, had tickled her. She smiled to herself. Smiled and smiled. Then she began to laugh.

He felt a fool.

Chapter Eighteen

The weather was unseasonably mild. He would have preferred some bite, even the savagery of a winter storm to strike at him, to reinstate some sense of himself as isolated and glad of it, which Katherine's visit had somehow weakened. He had read once in an Australian novel of a half-caste who had left his river town and 'gone bush': the phrase amused him when he applied it to himself, but the idea of someone disappearing into scrub, or in his case the woods, was still active in him, like something glowing and cave-like in his breast. He felt aware of the danger of losing touch with some mystery, of betraying it out of loneliness, or from being susceptible to the fragrance a woman can leave hanging in a room after she has left. In a kind of blind faith he turned back to the bristling darkness of the dank wood, feeling as he went into it that its paths were no longer willing to lead him anywhere.

One evening, still conscious of having to recover something precious he had mislaid, he sat at his table struggling to work. Nothing would flow. He got up and wandered about, and stood by the front window. He had picked up the local paper he had bought that morning in the village, rolling it up tight to beat against his leg. Stopping that, he opened it. His eyes went straying, out of morbidity or frustration, over the account of a suicide. Sitting down heavily in the jangly armchair he exclaimed aloud, 'Oh no.'

Julian McShane, the report said, had killed himself in the garage of his mother, the widow of Brigadier Henry McShane, by running a pipe from his van's exhaust to the van window. The gardener found him, opening the garage door to pick up some tools. The dead man had left notes to his mother and sister and to friends. He was in good health, under no strain that anyone was aware of, and had no debts. Friends who had seen him only the previous night in the *Golden Hind* spoke of his cheerful conversation. The paper described him as an unconventional character, well-liked in the town, who insisted on living his own life.

Hopkin, because he hardly knew the man, absorbed the shock of the news easily enough and believed he was not deeply affected. Then at night, waking in the small hours, he tossed about as if seeking to evade the waves of violence such an assault, so close, had caused, rocking through the atmosphere in wild radiations. After an hour, when he had given up attempts at getting back to sleep and was resigned to lying on his back and staring upwards, somehow he dropped off again.

Towards the end of the week Michael Symonds came by with a phone message. Would he contact a Katherine Wells when it was convenient?

'I know, yes,' Hopkin said. 'Thanks.'

'If you need to ring, use ours.'

'No, it's nothing urgent,' the tenant said hastily, irritated at having his private life, such as it was, exposed.

'No problems up here?'

'None I can think of.'

'Keeping warm?'

'Oh yes.'

Michael went off affably, full of energy and purpose. Hopkin envied him his physical tasks, his clear-cut day.

That evening he walked up to the village to make his call. Katherine answered at once. He was put off by her cagey tone, then when he identified himself he was startled again. She sounded tearful and low.

'What is it?' he asked.

'What's what?'

'You seem down in the mouth.'

'I'm all right,' she said defensively.

'Didn't you want to talk to me?'

'It doesn't matter. I shouldn't have bothered you. It's nothing.'

'You're not making sense.'

'It was just an impulse. Talking to you can't change anything.'

'Stop talking in riddles. Would you like me to come round?'

'If you like,' she said dully.
'Saturday morning?'
'If you've nothing better to do.'
'See you Saturday,' he said and rang off, surprised by his own decisiveness. He walked back troubled through the windy dark. Clearly the woman was unhappy about something. What was it? His imagination fed on the voice of someone frightened, turning this way and that to get away from something horrible, just as he had twisted and turned on his bed the other night.

Saturday he was there as promised, mid morning in bleak grey weather, the wind rasping at his cheeks and ears. It had gone cold. He understood that the street door was sometimes locked, and there was a grill for announcing yourself after ringing, which he hadn't noticed before. But she had left the door ajar for him.

She was there waiting at the top of the stairs and let him in without a word, unsmiling. Her appearance bewildered him, her head a mass of springy curls, earrings hanging low, that looked heavy. Also her hair was straw-coloured. He thought she looked drawn, introspectively unfocussed and suffering from strain. He wondered too if she had lost weight.

'Sit down,' she said, weary and evasive. 'Thanks for coming.' She stared at him almost resentfully.

'What's wrong?'

'Who said there was anything wrong?'

Not hearing his name used he felt distanced and cold, and had to swallow down his regret at coming. 'Are you sure this is a good idea?' he said.

'Why, what d'you mean?' she said angrily. She sat down facing him, with such a jolt that her earrings clinked. She jumped up again at once as if on springs. 'I'll make some coffee.'

'Only if you're joining me.'

'I'm living on the stuff.'

Cradling the mug between her hands seemed to comfort her, though she didn't drink from it. 'I had some ghastly news on Monday,' she said.

At first he thought she was referring to her son. 'Not – '

She read his mind. 'No, no, not Justin. A man I know, an old friend. Ex-lover, in fact.'

Hopkin sat listening, prepared to give whatever sympathy he could muster. 'Is he ill?'

'Dead.'

Her visitor shook his head. 'How did it happen?'

'Suicide.'

Then it dawned. 'Go on.'

She attempted the name, choked on it. She wrung her hands. 'I just can't believe it,' she said, put down her mug and wept.

'Julian McShane,' he said.

'It's awful.'

'I read it in the paper.'

'I don't understand.' She was crying again.

'I knew him, well, we met, had a talk once, back in the autumn.'

She was staring at him pop-eyed. He told her briefly how it had come about. 'Can you believe it?' she asked.

When he didn't answer she cried out again, 'Can you believe it?'

She was asking the blank walls, the furniture, not him. All he could think to say was, 'He seemed cheerful enough. Relaxed. He was kind to me in the pub, and after all I was a complete stranger.'

He was aware of babbling, of having nothing of importance to contribute, and told her so. She shook her head violently, jumped up and took her untouched coffee into the kitchen. He heard her pouring it away. She came back mopping her face with a tissue. 'It said in the paper that he left notes,' he remembered.

'One was for me.'

There it was on the coffee table, stained and crumpled. She thrust it at him.

'Are you sure you want me to?'

'Go on, read it.' Crying again, she waved her hand wildly.

He read unwillingly:

> Dear Katherine,
> I tried to contact you, I kept trying, though I had no right after we had been given our chance and failed. I blame you for nothing, I

blame nobody. Suddenly I've got to die, because it is all going to get worse and what is being offered to me and everybody is deadly poison. Have a drink on me. If only ....

'Clear as mud, wouldn't you say?' she said, shocking him with her bitter mockery.

'He didn't sign his name,' Hopkin began senselessly.

'He refused.'

'Refused?'

She seemed about to cry again but stopped herself. In a lifeless voice she said, 'Refused to go on.'

'Why?'

'Because that was him, what he was, always. The great refuser. On all fronts.'

Now she seemed in control and able to converse, he tried again. 'Tell me what you mean,' he coaxed.

Waiting for her to answer he was in trouble with his stomach. It might have been the note, the sudden brush with death, or the tension Katherine exuded. It was the first time he had read someone's last words. Taking deep breaths he struggled not to feel sick.

'Didn't you get that impression, when you talked to him?' she asked.

He considered, did his best to remember, while thinking that whatever he might say was of no consequence whatsoever. He was there to listen, to keep her company – or was it to keep her demons at bay?

'Certainly he cared,' he mused. 'He wasn't going along with what was being offered. He made that plain, and there it is in his note. He did say he couldn't live at home.'

He waited for her to enlarge on this, since she had known him intimately.

'He refused,' she said again, tonelessly, as if to herself.

'Was it a long relationship?'

'Oh, two years, on and off.'

'Was it difficult?'

'Bloody impossible.'

'Because of this position he'd taken up? What you call his refusal?'

She didn't seem to comprehend what he was saying. Words began pouring out of her. 'I'd got the phone unplugged, that's why he couldn't reach me. Oh, what have I done? I was feeling down, I'd been to the doctor, I was swallowing the bloody pills, it was Jimmy, I still hadn't got over Jimmy, I kept swallowing pills and all I got was chronic constipation and a mouth like the bottom of a budgie's cage, and the shakes, look!'

She held up her hands and he could see the tremor. Her expression was almost comic.

'So you're blaming yourself, is that it?'

'I don't know. Yes, yes!'

'All I can see at the moment is someone wallowing in self-pity.'

'Oh, piss off!'

'Believe me, I know what I'm talking about. I've done some wallowing in my time.' And he got up to go.

She buried her face in her hands and wept profusely. When he reached the door she cried out, 'Please, don't go! Don't leave me.'

'Am I any use to you? I wish I could be.'

He moved over to her and she stood up. They held on to each other. 'What should I do?' he asked, in humility but also confusion.

She recovered herself sufficiently to talk again in her normal voice. 'Do what you're best at,' she said.

She even smiled wanly. 'What's that?' he asked.

'Being here.'

'All right.'

She stopped smiling and was jeering miserably at herself. 'I let everybody down. I always have.'

'I don't believe you.'

'I do.'

'You haven't let me down.'

'Give me time.'

He decided to risk bringing back her crying jag. 'How did you let Julian down?'

'I've told you.'

'Not that. During your time with him. Was it your fault it ended? Doesn't it take two?'

She looked at him coldly, straight through him, as though not recognising him. 'He wanted me to think as he did. About everything. Loyalty, he called it.'

'You couldn't give it?'

She turned down her mouth. 'What's loyalty, when a man asks it, but another word for obedience?'

'So you couldn't give it,' he persisted.

'Never could, never will. Not to any man. Show me one who's worth it.'

'That's right,' he said. 'Have a kick at us instead of yourself.'

She almost smiled in spite of herself, so that he was lulled into thinking her immediate crisis was over.

He stayed on into the evening, wanting to leave and yet stay, veering around inside himself, unable to decide. She stood drawing the curtains on the dark, and seemed able to read his thoughts. When she turned there was abject fear on her face. 'Will you stay with me for a few days?' she blubbering piteously, the tears running down. 'Oh God, listen to me,' she moaned.

'You mean live here?'

'Just for a while. Will you?'

'Move in?' He was stalling, ashamed of his incredulous voice.

'Would that be so terrible?' She lashed at him bitterly: 'You could grit your teeth.'

He was sitting beside her on the sofa, wishing he was somewhere else. For the want of anything more practical he went on stroking and fiddling at her hair. He gave her his handkerchief to wipe her nose. He had his arm loosely about her, moved by her distress and wary of the contagion of her fright. After so many hours he was not far from hysteria himself. How to extricate himself without feeling a worm was the problem he was trying to solve.

They drank wine, which he thought would make her happier than her damned pills. Gradually he became aware of the cold gathering. When he asked about the storage heaters he realised she was fairly drunk and blurry. She was also out on her feet with fatigue. He thought if he could coax her into the bedroom and into bed he would be doing something useful. She made no objection. He took off her shoes and saw that her eyes were closed. About to turn away, he found she had a grip on his wrist.

'What?' he said softly.

She clung to him, speechlessly pleading. If he told the truth he was all in. He ended up beside her, seduced by the bed more than her, fully dressed at first. Soon the discomfort forced him to strip off, more or less. Then he was cold and wished he hadn't. Later, when Katherine lay on her back without stirring, he took off her skirt. In the light seeping through from the street lamps outside he could make out her defenceless face. He pitied her. Dropping off to sleep he sank away clutching handfuls of sheet around his shoulders. His last thought was that he should have kept on his shirt.

He woke with a jolt to find Katherine shaking from head to foot. Her right arm flailed about. He heard the bang as her hand struck the bedside table. Something went flying and hit the floor.

'Steady,' he croaked. She was like a landed fish thrashing in a boat.

'Warm me!' she moaned. 'It's cold! Lie on me.'

'Why is it freezing in here?'

'Please!'

He did as he was told in his befuddled state, scrambling over and squashing down on her as if she were a mattress. He was shivering himself. As their bodies shared the heat trapped between them he heard her moaning in the darkness, 'Say something to me!' Her wild beseeching entered his blood; his sex came alive. As he went into her, to the peace on earth he had found, he heard her still begging in her demented voice for words, to be told something, anything. It only made him more desirous, and thankful, more than he could have said, at being allowed into her soft body, which was like the warm body of life itself that he had been denied for so long, shivering and lost in the fields. Lying buried in stillness he heard the woman under him breathing heavily through the mouth and guessed she had passed out again. 'Lena,' he nearly whispered, as if he had come home to her or she to him.

He left as the light was breaking, sneaking out like a thief, the sky in grisly streaks of blood. He hesitated over leaving a note, failed to find a pen, and anyway what was there to say? He pacified his concern for her by telling himself he would be in touch, though God knows, he joked bleakly in his head, he had been pretty much in touch already.

He rang that same day, then on Sunday and Monday evening, the phone ringing senselessly. He thought of going back and jabbing her bell, felt scraggy with indecision and finally said to himself that if it was urgent he would be contacted. Tossing in disturbed sleep he woke up angry enough at one point to admit the truth, that he couldn't face another day like that one. Which was perhaps contemptible, certainly weak.

Unable to get Katherine's plight out of his head he finally went back, and walked about indecisively near her flat the following Saturday morning. On his second turn through the little web of streets he saw something which made him want to rub his eyes. There was Jimmy Plant, transformed by a sharp suit, letting himself in at the lower door next to the delicatessen: with a key.

Without understanding why, Hopkin was aware of anger fuelling his legs as he went after Jimmy's heels through the open door and up the stairs. At the flat door he lifted his hand to knock, pushed instead and walked in.

'Allo,' Jimmy said, showing no surprise. He was sprawled out on the sofa, reading a newspaper.

Hopkin mouthed his lie. 'I was looking for Katherine.'

'Out shoppin',' Jimmy said.

'How is she?'

'No idea, mate.' It sounded brutal, indifferent; the Jimmy he knew.

But not this apparition. The round wire-framed glasses were surely a new thing? He tried and failed to connect this spruce laid-back character with the taut scarecrow packed with the dynamite of his ugly truth crouching over his pages in the freezing shed. He remembered his rare gesture of a smile, the beautiful surprising teeth. The metamorphosis before him made no sense.

Still astonished, he asked, 'What about you?'

'Me?'

'Where are you living now?'

'Here, for a bit.'

'In the flat?'
'Kath asked me.'
'So you've heard about Julian?'
'That's why I'm here. She got in a state.'
'I know.'
Jimmy nodded vaguely. He touched his dry lips with his wet tongue. 'Poor ole Julian, eh,' he said, averting his eyes as if bored.
'You knew him?'
The house guest looked doubtful. 'We spoke a time or two. Not what you'd call knowing. He added meaningfully, 'Not like Kath.'

Hopkin said goodbye abruptly and left. On his way out he called over his shoulder. 'Tell Katherine I was here.' There was no answer and he'd expected none.

He'd intended to ask after the young writer's work, but the words stuck in his throat. It didn't help that his own writing had ground to a halt.

On his journey back he made up his mind to find out somehow whether Katherine was all right, but only after Jimmy Plant had served his purpose, whatever that was, and gone. Back in his hiding hole he played some Bach, a late passion, on a cheap Japanese cassette player he had purchased one day in an impulse. All he owned by the composer on tape were the two volumes of Cello Suites. They were inexhaustible, performed by Onczay on unaccompanied cello, intricate and simple at once like the woods beyond his walls. He sat on and on listening to this effulgence of a man's spirit, until the questions knotting in his nerves were set free and woven. He was lifted up, and afterwards sat quietly in a sort of trance. It took some time to understand what had changed. He had begun to feel better about himself.

Chapter Nineteen

All at once, before he knew it he was in February, deep in winter darkness still but with a sense of that envisioned springtime racing towards him underground in a great surge. This subterranean force, experienced as wild rumour in the tree of his veins, was what sustained him he believed when he was in danger of slipping into a lack of faith in himself, trudging on because there was no alternative. Like his mother, he thought mournfully.

One murky afternoon he was going past the farmhouse and Mr Symonds called him in. Was he hankering after company like me, he wondered. No, the messianic farmer with a belly the other envied, it looked so robust, all meat and purpose, wanted to engage the ex-lecturer in conversation about his least favourite subject, education. Or if not talk to him, talk at him. He sat his tenant down at the huge scrubbed table in the draughty kitchen, near a Rayburn radiating warmth.

'We'll have a fall of snow in the night,' he announced.

'Is it that cold?' Hopkin asked.

'Doesn't have to be. We won't get much, a sprinkling is my guess.'

Hopkin was excited at the thought. To rise after a night's sleep and look out, astounded by a silently transformed world, would swing him straight into childhood, as well as be a metaphor for the kind of alchemy promised by art.

Symonds had been reading a biography of Alan Paton. It had fired him up. Now his ugly, open face was alight with what he'd discovered in it. 'Did you know he was a teacher, then principal of the worst black borstal in South Africa for fifteen years, and in the end president of the Liberal Party there? Know that?'

Hopkin confessed his ignorance. 'All I know of him is that one famous novel of his.'

Getting into his stride, Symonds said, 'It's unbelievable what he did with that borstal, turning it into a humane reformatory against all the odds. Naturally he was too successful for his own good. After the war he locked horns with Verwoerd over apartheid. Well, you know all that. I was put off by his puritanism, not that we don't all have our own versions, but it's not pretty to read about – and by his use of corporal punishment. That was the era he came from of course, and his own father was a hideous old flogger, so there you are.'

What struck Hopkin once again about this man was his love of talking for its own sake, spilling out words in gushes without waiting for a response. This was his passion, perhaps even more than organic farming. The function of speech itself possessed him. Did his wife's profound deafness have anything to do with it? Hopkin was impressed again by this remarkable man's scope, talking with easy familiarity about the ideas of Homer Lane, Eleanor Gleuck, Cyril Burt, ranging to and fro at will. If the subject happened to be art he was equally at home, as he was with music and literature. On the shelves of his cavernous sitting room were sumptuous art folios, in the corner a grand piano. He was a fluent pianist. He combined delicacy with the rudeness of a savage; they lived seemingly at ease in the one clumsy body. He tended to bulldoze and demand agreement, condemning outright those he saw as wrong-minded or hypocritical. Hopkin, an admirer in spite of himself, wasn't blind to the man's rampant egotism. Symonds was both despot and crusader, unable to help himself. He asked Hopkin if he thought education in this country was a lost cause.

Struggling to answer, the quiet listener was taken aback by his own pessimism. 'Family life is shaky,' he ventured, 'the father can't command respect as mine did, in fact nothing much today is really respected or believed in. The low status of teachers is no surprise, surely? But why look to education for answers when they're scratching their heads like everyone else, and politicians are just ducking below the parapet – when society as a whole is coming apart at the seams?'

Symonds, in everything he said and did a straight-from-the-shoulder man, wanted to know what could be done. 'Apart from kicking this discredited lot out, that is. Labour?' Rushing on powerfully he said, 'Look, if the young are denied social significance – to use Paton's phrase – they rapidly degenerate, end up as thugs, hoodlums, layabouts, yobbos, delinquents of one sort or another. If the world looks bleak, black, meaningless, they'll find another, take off with drugs, liquor, crime. Isn't that so? Paton was talking about young blacks, I'm talking about our own youth, black and white alike.'

'What was his answer then?'

'Paton? Simple. No use reforming prisons, education, this or that, you have to devise a programme aimed at a reform of the whole of society, root and branch.'

Hopkin talked back, hearing his own vague call for a new vision and disliking it, unable to see a sign of one anywhere. 'Maybe we need to be plunged into some catastrophe in order to wake up and do something. Education was the rallying call once, not any more. Am I being cynical?'

Symonds glared at him like an enraged bull. A supremely practical man, he was hardly likely to embrace apocalypse. The phone rang out in the passage and he left the kitchen. Hopkin seized his chance and slipped away. Talk like this always left him oppressed with a feeling of futility. Symonds was right, but so what? How did one act? Where was there anyone not greedily preoccupied with his own affairs, nose in the trough? Hadn't it all gone too far, become too corrupt, in that insidious English fashion that looks on the outside so nice and decent, till you bit into it? There was nothing rotten about Symonds, for all his monomania: he was sound all through, ruddy as an apple, Hopkin thought to himself, walking away disgruntled to his safe house. There he sat in the dark for a while, trying to recover a sense of himself. Finally he sat dreaming of snow.

No naturalist, he missed details but noticed the strange bodilessness of the thinned-out woods, the transparency of the air, the way in which sounds travelled further. The sky seemed higher and yet as if conversing with the earth. He laughed at his own fancy: all the same it was something. In his journal he used the word clarity to express it. The country surrounding him was stripped and opened out. So was his life. Instead of feeling he was on the threshold of old age and near the end he had the sensation of looking forward into vast distances.

The death in nature was unavoidable, yet it carried you forward like a tide towards the spring. What about his own coming death? What about Lena's? Entering the woods, aware of their strange winter pallor, swept by cold draughts of wind, he felt bleached with cold and deathly himself and so able to believe almost without thinking that the dead were all around him somewhere.

Immediately after his wife's death he had been distraught enough to believe in ghosts, or at least to want to. He was so desperate to raise her from the dead that he wanted his own life to diminish, to be less, as if by giving up his own substance he could transfer it, by the awful force of his grief, to her.

One day near mid March he was sorting through some old papers and came on his words to her across the chasm of death. The loss rose up again unbearably from the paper as he read: 'Where are you my darling, where have you gone, how could I have let it happen?' He wept as he read on and his eyes blurred, as all the progress he had been making on the journey across his immense Siberia was blotted out, lost in the blizzard of his loss. 'Take me with you, please, please. You *have* taken me, I'm not here any more, this isn't me, this dried-up obscenity of a thing, sucked of warm blood and left here to go on existing. My love, my love.'

These days he found no difficulty in believing in ghosts, though he had never been haunted and stopped longing to be. He believed in them as guides or spirits watching over us, taking us by the hand invisibly, leading us in one direction when we might have taken another. In his other life, before coming here, he would have scoffed at this.

And something curious was happening inside him, flinging him about, making him want to act, to go racing off somewhere. In the grip of this acute restlessness he had a letter from Bill Walsh, giving a new address. He had moved with Marie into Plymouth, to a basement flat near Central Park. 'This bloody cellar,' he called it, 'crawling with woodlice in all the corners.' He wrote violently, chaotically, desperate as ever, hinting darkly at a coming catastrophe. 'It can't go on like this, we both know it, Marie says it's intolerable, meaning me, I want her to leave but she won't abandon me, I want to go myself but she's my lifebuoy, that's why I hate her, could throttle her, what a filthy mess ....' He spoke of his paintings in terms of dread, seeing portents in them which were terrible warnings of something murderous about to happen. 'One is so loathsome I've turned it to the wall, a self-portrait naturally but it's the *truth* and I've got this mad urge to drag it out into the street in this benighted town and show everybody what kind of life we're living here, what everybody's living, that's it, their rotten grovelling secrets....'

Instead of putting him off, the words filled Hopkin with an even stronger urge to go there and then and tell his trapped friend the story of his last six months, or was that being as mad as Bill sounded? If he did go, if Bill allowed him to come, would he be willing to sit there and say nothing, with this new power to endure and survive sitting inside him? If so, Bill would pick up on it in a flash with his sharpened malice and find him detestable. And six months ago he would have felt the same, when his misanthropy was virulent.

He imagined the scene, a repeat of scenes he had experienced before on visits to Bill, the mask-like falsely smiling face confronting him at the door, taut with the effort to be civil, watching him with vindictive eyes, jealous of his recovered state. He would say afterwards to Marie, 'Christ, that bastard, how he always falls on his feet!' Still, Hopkin thought he would risk it. It had nothing to do with duty or with pity. The bond between them was weak now but it still held. The idea of it was no longer dangerous to him. He was surprised by his new steadiness. Was he trying to test himself? No, he was intact again and it didn't matter where he went, he was free to move about at will. His hiding place was somehow redundant. It had served him well, he had come to love it, but the truth was he had no need to hide, not any more. As for Bill, he hadn't seen his friend for over three years, and what they had once meant to each other ran deep. All right, it was the worst possible time, but is there ever a right time? He thought he would go.

One evening, the time of day when his emotional life would gather most strongly in his chest, he castigated himself for being revived by the friendship with Katherine Wells. It was better to stay chaste: in a way he still was. He stood accused, but of what? The truth was that his slow renewal of feeling and his frail candle-flame conviction that he would be reunited with whatever might nourish him if he only had patience and some courage, and could hold out and wait, this had come before his meeting with Katherine, not after. Proof of this lay in the poems he had written. He had kept faith with the dead and been rewarded.

Eager to clarify his meditations he got up next morning and began a poem which grew steadily bigger. Writing it he experienced moments of anguish, remembering imaginary conversations he would have with his wife on walks, when she called him by name and drew intolerably close, and all the time he went on with his work of the spirit. There had been so much weeping, such brokenness: was he in a fit state to mend *anything*? He felt himself to be no more than the fulcrum for what he had set in motion, which he thought of as 'What the Trees Tell', and then simply 'Evergreens'.

He had travelled a long bitter road already from the deathly cold place he had crawled into after his wife's death, excoriated by a crime no one else would recognise. His induction into a terrible coldness began with an embrace by something that put an end to any possibility of human warmth. That was what he deserved, what he wanted to suffer: to be taken out of his body, drained of blood, severed from the living. He remembered Lawrence's poem in anticipation of his own death, where he speaks of being left with 'only the leavings of a life'.

He wrote at full stretch, the tears in his eyes partly self-pity and also thankfulness at being given this release, in charge of his demons and in touch with her, the woman he had married and known truly naked, to whom he would always look for guidance, in the sky or in the big unconscious landscape, deep in thickets or trees or wherever she was, as she accompanied his every step. Trying for the deep sorrowful note which would always sound now behind the silvery bugles of birds with their bubbling newness, he opened at one point his copy of *Leaves of Grass*, a book he kept near at hand, glancing at tear-swollen lines that were beautiful but not his.

He carried on churning out one revised version after another until he was in danger of losing faith. He sat there thinking he would probably give up writing poems for good. What else was there to say?

He got up in a daze and cut thick doorstops of bread, filling a sandwich with beetroot which when he handled and sliced it reminded him of liver.

Going back again to read what he had made he was at first bewildered, then exhilarated as the plain words took possession of him. It was a death poem, saying over and over that there was no death. Was he embracing Christ's message, did he believe in a kingdom one entered which made death no more than a word? He had written 'The dead are living with us', and the lament became a rhapsody for the dead 'manifold as rain', and there was his wife speaking through the evergreens 'to one side somewhere'.... 'in the soft secrecy of dank woods'. This was a message sent to him by Lena or he was hopelessly deluded. So he thought, before a wave of utter tiredness swamped him. He fought an urge to lie down. Lost in his words, he couldn't decide on anything. He went on reading and reading until the meaning, which he'd thought was as clear as day, sank away from him.

As the night gathered and pressed at the windows he went to the bathroom to pass water and was shocked when he emitted a bloody stream, forgetting what he had been eating. Relieved, he laughed out loud, hearing the slightly hysterical edge.

In the kitchen boiling water for tea he thought he heard a faint humming. He cut the switch and listened intently, heart banging. Only the night playing tricks on him, he told himself.

In spite of all his waiting and longing, in the end he was caught out by the spring. Suddenly he was surrounded, in another world. It lay all around him, its signature on all things. In his solitary, over-excited state it hit him like a clap of revelation. It was how he imagined it might be in the heart of Russia when the ice suddenly broke and the waters flowed. Inside him the ice splintered with a deafening crack. Spellbound, he penetrated the cold wood that was still stagnant with winter, coming on his first clump of thick-clustered primroses by accident, without even looking. They were only half in the world, half-unfurled, perhaps fearful of showing blanched lemony faces among the rusty strands of bramble. A shiver of delight ran through him, as if they were his own creation.

Spirit of the Woods

He went through the dripping trees on another day and became conscious of the birdsong intensifying. Trees had grown beautiful with potency, finding things to say in their new freedom, now they were not dumb with cold. You believed it was possible to hear the naked limbs of maples, sycamores and beeches disentangling themselves from sleep. Ghostly presences as well as birds called with the voice of life, in the common language shared by life and death. Celandines, new-minted and varnished, lay back wide open and ardent, dandelions studding the rough turf in front of the cottage with yellow stars, jumping up more thickly each day.

By the end of April it was in full swing, great pools of bluebells lifting clear of the new heads of curled baby bracken. It was almost too much; he drowned in riches. Nothing he wrote could ever match this ancient triumph. He gave up trying.

Reeling with all this beauty on earth he set out to visit his friend Bill, whose sick psyche he had once feared.